THERE IS NO *You and I*

JESS SINGH

INDIA • SINGAPORE • MALAYSIA

ISBN
Paperback 979-8-89699-283-7
Hardcase 979-8-89724-777-6

Contents

For You......

You know?
I love you.
That smile of yours,
It's one of my favorite things.

You know?
Those eyes of yours,
When they look at me?
Something courses through my veins,
An electric shock,
A fast wave,
Making my heart race.

Else?

Who knows?

It's just a body,

A walking dead,

Until your presence

Breathes life into me,

Fueled by your visits,

Awakening the dormant soul.

In your gaze, I find my spark,

In your smile, I feel my light,

For in this dance of love,

I am still alive.

Cocaine

In the vibrant, pulsating heart of a Mumbai nightclub, where the beats thumped and laughter mingled with chatter, Raghav and Manav slipped into the washroom, cloaked in secrecy and exhilaration. Tonight promised thrills, and they were eager to partake in a risky rendezvous with a powdery substance. "Crush it with the card," Raghav instructed, his voice low. "Pass me your card," Manav replied, carefully unwrapping a white rock from a small plastic package.

His freshly manicured hands made the task a bit tricky, but he was determined. "Dude, how did you even sneak this in?" Raghav asked, retrieving his saddle-stitched leather wallet and handing over a credit card. The white rock was soon laid out on the toilet seat in the brightly lit washroom, the music of Yo Yo Singh blasting through the walls. Two bodyguards in black stood sentinel outside, while the lights from the dance floor flickered across the blue ceramic tiles, adding to the chaotic ambience. "How long are you even in the country? Two months a year? Sneaking stuff in must be easy," Manav replied, beginning to crush the rock into a fine powder.

Mumbai never truly slept; even in the early morning hours, the city buzzed with life. The stories of last night were etched in the eyes of its inhabitants, often hidden behind dark sunglasses under the bright sun. At 1:00 am, the washroom was bustling. "I'm making two lines for now," Manav said, snorting one and leaving the other for Raghav. Both of them were barely upright, but the party had to go on. "Damn, this is good shit," Raghav exclaimed, running his fingers through his hair, attempting to fix his dishevelled look. "Yeah, but you know what's hard? Getting out of this washroom," Manav said, glancing around the cramped stall while the bodyguards waited outside.

Raghav bent over to snort the last bit of powder with a 1000-rupee bill, raising an eyebrow. "And why's that?" "Because someone's going to think we're in here getting it on," Manav joked, rubbing his nostril. Raghav shrugged, watching Manav with a smirk. "So, what if they think we're gay? It's not the 1980s. If we are, then we are." "If it were the '80s, we'd be getting mocked," Manav chuckled. They finally stepped out of the washroom, the bodyguards falling into step behind them. The two men approached the bar, where their friends Kavya and Shubhani were sipping martinis. "Hey, man! Get us all shots, will you? Shubhani's first film just launched!" Raghav exclaimed, joining them. "Yeah, Shubhani, we're all so proud of you!" Kavya said, wrapping her arms around Shubhani in a warm hug.

Four bodyguards dressed in casual blue jeans and shirts stood watch nearby. Kavya, clad in a short floral strapless dress and her favourite Jimmy Choo sandals, felt the weight of her bodyguards curbing her fun. She rolled her eyes. "Some days, I just wish I could make these guys disappear!" she muttered in frustration, taking a sip of her drink. Her voice was barely audible over the pounding music. "Did you see all the comments on Instagram under your movie page?" Kavya asked, scrolling through her iPhone 15 Pro, her brows furrowing. "I did, babes. Let's just enjoy our drinks for now," Shubhani replied, pulling out a black Chanel lip gloss and applying it to her lips.

"She's a product of nepotism," Raghav scoffed, reading the comments. "She's so dark!" "Oh, she looks just like her mother, but will she be a star too?" Fire emojis – 3 heart emojis, puke emojis … "She looks anorexic. Please start eating before you die." "Hot babe. You, my girlfriend? Plz?" "Sexy mom, ugly daughter." Raghav glanced at Shubhani, shaking his head. "Wow, people are so limited in their thinking."

"Blah, blah, blah. I'm just happy to be vacationing in Italy for a week. Babe, you're freaking awesome," Manav said, getting up to hug Shubhani. "Thank you, my love. You know, even with your nose ring, black nails, kajal-lined eyes, and blue mohawk, I still love you," Shubhani said, enveloping him in a tight embrace. "It's my rapper look, bro. You attract what you look like," Manav replied, ruffling his blue-haired mohawk. "You know, a doctor's kid can be a doctor, a mithai wala's son can run a sweet shop, an accountant's kid can become an accountant. But when an actor's child becomes an actor? That's a big deal," Raghav remarked, taking a swig of his whisky. "Dude, forget those comments. You're gorgeous," Kavya said, raising her glass. They all clinked their drinks together, the sound cutting through the thick air of the club. "Aree, when our uncles and aunties made it this far, so can you," Raghav encouraged. "Of course! More than half of India can't afford Netflix or Amazon Prime subscriptions. What choice do they have?" Manav laughed, downing his drink in one go. Kavya sipped her mojito, listening to her friends. "Forget about it, guys. I'm just 20, and the whole of India is on my case, bashing my skills and looks. These people need to get a life!" Shubhani exclaimed, taking a sip of her "Sex on the Beach" martini. The effects of the alcohol made the four of them lively, their voices rising above the pulsating music of the nightclub.

Emergency

Kavya adjusted her beaded red dress, which sat just above her knees, as she settled into the plush high chair at the bar. The brass chair, upholstered in rich olive-green velvet, hugged her form perfectly. Above the bar island hung a quirky mid-century modern pendant light, its bold gold finish casting a glamorous glow.

This bar had likely heard countless stories worthy of page-three gossip. "Kavya, guess what? You're next in line to be launched!" Shubhani exclaimed, raising her glass to clink against Kavya's. "Why can't we just dance? And no, I'm not getting launched. While everyone else is talking about sending their kids off for higher education or getting married, here we are, stepping into our parents' careers. It's not like we're selling Aloo Bhaji!" Kavya burst out, frustration was evident in her voice. "That's

Bollywood for you. We sell love stories, even if we don't always live them ourselves," Raghav quipped, rubbing his nostrils. "Yeah, let's go dance! You guys are so boring!" Shubhani said, grabbing Kavya's hand.

The four friends made their way to the dance floor, excitement bubbling among them. They danced under the pulsating music, lights flashing in vibrant colours as the atmosphere buzzed with energy. Raghav pulled out some mushrooms, passing them around. The DJ spun tracks at the helm, keeping the crowd euphoric beneath the laser lights, while a fog machine enveloped the room in an immersive haze. Kavya, Raghav, Manav, and Shubhani let loose, moving to the beat and losing themselves in the rhythm. The music thumped loudly, and the flashing neon lights created a kaleidoscope of colours. Their laughter mingled with the music, and they felt untouchable, lost in the crowd. Suddenly, a loud "thud" interrupted the revelry. Shubhani lay motionless on the dance floor, her Gucci purse sprawled beside her.

The music and lights continued, but Raghav, Manav, and Kavya stopped dancing, panic washing over them as they rushed to Shubhani's side. They knelt beside her, attempting to rouse her, but she remained unresponsive. Bodyguards quickly intervened, lifting Shubhani from the floor and carrying her outside as the security team assisted. Raghav called for his driver, and the BMW pulled up in front of the club.

Raghav, barely able to stand, shouted at a nearby photographer, snatching the camera and throwing it to the ground. "Stop, you dumbass! This isn't something you want to take pictures of!" His drunkenness made him unsteady as one of his bodyguards pulled him back. The BMW SUV was there, and the bodyguard practically shoved Raghav into the car. Kavya, still in shock, climbed into the Lexus SUV with Shubhani, and the driver sped off towards the hospital.

A black Range Rover pulled up to the club entrance, and Manav managed to hop in. "Follow them to the hospital," he instructed his driver. "Here's some water, Manav," the driver, in his late 40s, passed him a bottle from the inbuilt fridge. "Isn't it weird and sad, Rajiv?" Manav mused, taking a sip of water and leaning back against the seat. "What's that, Manav Sir?" the driver replied, keeping his eyes focused on the road. "Imagine if we're not dying from drugs or malnutrition, this judgemental audience in India will kill us anyway," Manav said, sinking into the seat. Silence filled the SUV as the gravity of their situation settled in.

"You'll be fine, Shubhani," Kavya murmured, gently rubbing her friend's forehead. But her own intoxication made it hard to keep her head straight. She scanned the car for something to vomit in, finally opening her small black Givenchy mini Antigona bag and losing her stomach into it.

Wiping her face with a tissue, she leaned her head against the window, watching as streetlights blurred into a continuous stream of light. The mushrooms were kicking in, distorting her reality. The traffic in Mumbai never slept. Ironically, the BMW couldn't speed them along; the traffic remained relentless. Shubhani lay unconscious in the back seat, and after what felt like an eternity, the three cars finally arrived at the hospital. They halted outside the hospital entrance as bodyguards carried Shubhani inside. Raghav, Kavya, and Manav stumbled out of their SUVs, still intoxicated, and leaned on their bodyguards for support as they walked into the hospital. They waited anxiously outside the room where Shubhani was being treated, watching as doctors and nurses rushed around her, hooking her up to an IV.

After what felt like half an hour, a doctor emerged, looking serious but relieved. "Shubhani is stable for now. It appears she hasn't eaten anything, and fainting was a result of drinking on an empty stomach," he informed the three friends, who were slumped on a couch in the upscale hospital. "Where are her parents? We need some signatures or an adult guardian," the doctor asked, looking at them expectantly. "No, just a credit card.

Her parents are filming in Singapore," Raghav replied, trying to maintain eye contact despite his intoxication. "It's okay. We'll figure this out. You guys can go home. She'll be in our care for the next few hours," the doctor reassured them before walking away. Silence fell among the three friends as they processed the night's events, each lost in their own thoughts while they waited for Shubhani to recover.

Helicopter Child

"Kavya, how is Shubhani now? Have you called her?" Kavya's father, Amar, settled into a brown leather lounge chair, the ocean breeze flowing through the large glass sliding doors, tousling his long hair. He held a Hermès H Deco cup and saucer, sipping his coffee thoughtfully.

"No, Dad. Not yet," Kavya replied, scrolling through her phone, lost in her social media feed. "Kavya, Shubhani has been in the hospital for 13 hours. You really should check on her," Amar insisted, placing his cup on the white saucer. He slipped his feet into his black Bottega Veneta slippers and rose from the chair. "Daddy, she'll be fine."

All Shubhani needs is some food before she disappears. She's trying so hard to be thin for the sake of ignorant people," Kavya continued scrolling, barely looking up. Sounds of loud music and chatter spilt from her phone as notifications chimed. "Or maybe you kids should consider cutting back on the partying and focus on something more constructive," Amar suggested, his voice calm but firm. A Bollywood star in his 50s, he had a well-built physique. He wore a white robe, with salt-and-pepper hair on his chest hinting at maturity.

"When do we even party, Dad? We're either at film festivals or charity functions, or we're jetting off to some vacation spot where no one knows us. Sometimes, it's nice to be incognito," Kavya set her phone down and looked at him. "Darling, I'm not trying to stop you from having fun. I'm just suggesting moderation," Amar replied, raising an eyebrow. "Moderation? In what sense? I just told you we're hardly ever here. So how can we party in moderation?" Kavya rolled her eyes. Amar picked up a newspaper and opened to Page 3. "Kavya, you need to speak to your father with more respect. This isn't how you should communicate," he said, glancing at her while she remained unbothered. Asha, Kavya's mother, focused on setting the breakfast table.

"Oh, my goodness, it's getting hot in here. Can we all sit at the breakfast table? That's a rare occasion!" she said, wrapped in a green silk saree, gold bangles jingling on her arms and a diamond bracelet on her left wrist. Her hair was neatly tied up in a bun. A man in black pants and a white shirt, their butler Numan, stood beside a trolley filled with coffee and juices. "No, Mum. I'm okay," Kavya replied, hugging her mother. "You're always so sweet, Mum."

Asha ensured the dining table was perfectly arranged. "Numan, please bring out the fruit salad tray; it's missing," Kavya smiled at Numan, who had served them for 16 years. "That suit looks great on you, Numan uncle." "Thank you, dear. Come have breakfast; I made your favourite chicken cutlets," he said, pulling out a chair for her. He then grabbed a fruit salad plate and handed it to Asha. The three of them sat at the large dining table, the ocean breeze drifting in through the open doors of their Mumbai mansion. "Darling Amar, you have a flight to catch in two hours," Asha reminded him as she filled her floral ceramic plate with fruit. The dining table, set for 12, was filled with silence, only interrupted by the faint sound of music playing on the gramophone.

"I warned Chaitali to send Shubhani to Oxford. What kind of mother subjects her child to this world? Shubhani isn't pretty; she has a dark complexion. She wouldn't even get an ad for a fairness cream. And Chaitali launched her in a film?" Asha spoke without making eye contact. "How can you say that, Mum? She's my friend! We grew up together!" Kavya's anger flared. "Darling, I'm just being honest," Asha insisted, focusing on her breakfast. "Plus, we're launching you in a movie next year, so you should understand the reality," Amar added, placing chicken cutlets on his plate and drizzling sauce over them. "Okay, I'm done here. I'm not going to be part of any movie or your projects. I'm moving to New York tomorrow," Kavya declared, pushing her plate away and standing up. "And who said you could do that?" Amar's gaze sharpened as he looked directly at her. "I said it, Dad!" In her frustration, Kavya knocked over a Balcon du Guadalquivir vase—a precious gift she had bought for Amar last year for nearly $1,900. The vase, adorned with 24-carat gold thread, shattered on the floor. "Kavya!" Amar's voice rose, disbelief washing over him. "She's right, Amar. She'll enjoy life in New York. Plus, Mia is there. They can look out for each other, and my sister lives there too," Asha chimed in, trying to mediate. Kavya stood in the middle of the luxurious living room, which boasted posh white couches and a stunning view of the ocean.

Amar stepped closer to her, embracing her and kissing her forehead. Kavya pushed him away again, retreating to the window. "I'm sick of pretending to be happy 24/7 when I'm not!" she yelled, her voice echoing in the spacious room. "What more do you want? You have the best life—vacations around the world, everything at your fingertips. So stop complaining, Kavya," Amar shot back, frustration evident. "Really, Daddy? Do you know how many times you asked me to smile for your

Instagram photos? Every time I step outside, there are strangers with cameras flashing in my face, even at night. It feels like I'm living in a jail with surveillance on me 24/7!" Kavya's composure cracked, revealing the weight of her reality.

She was a striking girl with long black hair, sharp features, and a delicate frame, often resembling a character straight out of a fairy tale. "There are other star kids who don't have this problem. Look at Rahul and Ravya; they enjoy it. What's your issue, Kavya?" Amar questioned, raising an eyebrow. "I hate living like a helicopter child. I want to be free and live like normal kids do." In her anger, Kavya knocked another vase down, this one worth over £2,000. "Are you saying you want to work and earn your own money like regular people do? Can you live without this luxury?" Amar laughed, almost dismissively, as he took another bite of his breakfast.

Kavya fell silent, her heart racing. Asha, wrapped in her saree, stood quietly, caught in the crossfire between her daughter and her celebrity husband. "Dad, what part of this don't you understand? I can't even run away from home because everyone knows me. It's suffocating here. I want to breathe and live freely, to eat in a restaurant with friends, without anyone watching. I'm tired of posing for you and doing everything for Instagram!" Kavya's voice wavered, her frustration spilling over. "Sweetheart, most people would kill to be in your shoes," Amar said softly, stepping closer to her and grasping her arms, trying to connect. "Daddy, please. Can I just once try to live like that? What's the harm? I might learn something," she pleaded, her tone calmer as she looked into his eyes. "Okay, fine. If you want to live normally, you'll have to earn your own money. You can go live in our apartment in New York, find a job, and don't call me for anything. You have to find your own path," Amar relented, walking out of the room.

Asha and Kavya stood alone, the tension lingering in the air. Numan began clearing away the untouched breakfast, the only sound breaking the heavy silence. "Happy?" Asha asked, looking at Kavya. Kavya nodded, tears brimming in her eyes, and wrapped her arms around her mother in a tight embrace.

Six Months Later

February 14th

It was 6 am in New York City, the bustling sounds of the city echoing through the night. Yet in her penthouse, Kavya found herself cocooned in silence. The only sound piercing the tranquillity was the persistent ringing of her phone. Reluctantly, she emerged from her warm blanket and reached for her phone. It was February 14th.

"Hello?" Kavya mumbled, still half-asleep. "Happy birthday, baby!" her mother exclaimed, her voice bright and cheerful from the other end. "Thanks, Mum. But it's 6 am," Kavya replied, rolling back into her bed, trying to block out the morning. "It's 6:30 pm here! I thought you would be awake. Happy birthday, my little doll, and happy Valentine's Day!" her mother continued, unperturbed by the time difference. "Thanks, Mum. You're being funny," Kavya said, her eyes still closed.

"How's Mia? You two girls behaving?" her mother asked, curiosity lacing her tone. "We're good, Mum. Mia is doing well," Kavya reassured her, finally tossing aside the blanket and sitting up. Her spacious white bed and plush comforter faced the window, where a clear, dark sky revealed a few twinkling stars, their brilliance dulled by the vibrant lights of New York City. "Okay, darling. Your birthday present is waiting for you downstairs. I suggest you go check with your building doorman," her mother urged. "Mum, I'm going back to sleep. I have a party tonight," Kavya said, pulling the blanket back over her face in annoyance. "Well, I think you should go take a look at what your mum and dad sent you!" "Fine, Mum. I'll walk downstairs."

Kavya begrudgingly slipped into her silk nightgown, wrapped herself in a robe, and opened her bedroom door, making her way to the second floor. The penthouse was on the 88th floor, and as she walked through the living room with its impressive 15-foot ceilings and white couches, she couldn't help but admire the breathtaking view of downtown and the East River. It was like living in a fishbowl, but right now, it felt empty and lonely. As she headed to the elevator, she could faintly hear the sound of an ambulance in the distance. She took the elevator down to the lobby.

The lobby featured stunning murals and a mosaic floor. This high-end apartment building boasted a designer couch and an elaborate chandelier hanging in the centre. Kavya approached the reception desk. "Good morning, madam. How can I help you?" the receptionist inquired. "Do I have a parcel delivery? I'm here to pick up a gift my mother sent for my birthday. I'm Kavya from the penthouse on the 88th floor."

She was still in her robe and fuzzy slippers. "Oh, happy birthday, madam! Your birthday present has been delivered. You're one lucky girl," the receptionist replied with a smile. "Thank you!" she said, feeling a flicker of excitement. "Please see Liam, the doorman. He'll guide you to your gift," he instructed. Kavya walked towards the revolving doors, where a tall man stood waiting. Liam, dressed in a blue uniform and hat, towered over her. His pants sat just below his belly, and he wore polished black shoes. "Good morning, madam. How may I assist you?" Liam greeted her.

"I'm here for a gift?" she said, still feeling a bit muddled and sleepy. "A gift for Kavya?" Liam checked his register. "Yes," she confirmed. "Happy birthday, ma'am! Please follow me to the parking garage," he said, motioning for her to follow. "Parking garage? I thought it would be delivered to my door," Kavya replied, confusion washing over her as she looked around the reception area for a birthday parcel and found nothing. She shook her head and followed Liam. They walked to the underground parking lot, where Kavya spotted a truck parked. Still unsure of what was happening, she watched as Liam retrieved a red velvet box and handed it to her. Then, her eyes widened as she saw a brand-new red convertible BMW parked in her designated spot.

As she opened the door, a cascade of red and white balloons spilt out of the car, filling the air with a festive spirit. Kavya quickly fished out her phone and dialled her mother's number. "Thank you, Mum! I love this beautiful gift!" she exclaimed. The balloons continued to float around her as Liam began to turn to leave. "Sorry, doorman! I made a mess!" Kavya yelled after him. "Not a problem, ma'am. I'll clean it up. Congratulations, ma'am! You're a very lucky girl," he replied with a smile as he walked away. Kavya hopped into the car, ignited the engine, and took it for a spin through the vibrant streets of New York City. Her phone rang again, and she picked it up. "Happy birthday, sister! Are you not in your room?" Mia asked with a hint of surprise.

"I'm taking a spin in the city. I'm still in my robe, but I should be home in about five minutes," Kavya replied, her excitement bubbling over. "Okay, but my car keys are at home. What are you driving?" Mia questioned. "Mom and Dad sent me a BMW for my birthday!" Kavya beamed.

"You brat! See you soon at home. We can go for a spin together later," Mia said before hanging up. New

York City felt alive and ever-moving. The tall buildings seemed to race against one another, striving to touch the sky. The streets were packed even at this early hour, a rush of life all around her. Kavya, sitting in her new BMW, watched as people bustled about, completely unaware of her presence. It was liberating! Had she been in India, stepping out in a robe would have made headlines, but here, in New York, she was just another face in the crowd. A smile spread across her face as she took a U-turn, embracing the freedom of her new life.

The Dildo is Fine!

"Doorman, could you please help me park this car?" Kavya asked as she arrived at the entrance of her building, the gleaming red convertible BMW catching the eye of passersby.

"Of course, madam," Liam, the doorman, replied, taking the keys from her hand. Still clad in her robe and fuzzy slippers, Kavya shielded her eyes with oversized sunglasses, her hair tousled but undeniably chic in a carefree way. The building was busier than usual this morning with a flurry of activity around her. As she walked through the lobby and entered the elevator, she noticed other residents but felt a sense of anonymity. No one seemed to care that she was in a robe; that was the beauty of New York City—everyone was too preoccupied with their own lives to pay attention to anyone else.

Inside the elevator, she quickly scanned the faces. A tall Caucasian man in a navy blue suit stood in the corner, clutching a black briefcase adorned with the logo of Stefano Ricci. His Gucci eyeglasses reflected the faint overhead lighting, and although she couldn't see his face, the salt-and-pepper hair neatly parted to the side suggested maturity and authority. The other occupants of the elevator stood in stony silence as if they were mannequins frozen in time.

For a fleeting moment, Kavya missed the vibrant energy of India, where people were more expressive and engaged. The elevator chimed, and she stepped out onto the 88th floor, making her way into the penthouse. Kavya jumped onto the plush couch, almost spilling Mia's coffee as she wrapped her arms around her sister in a tight embrace. "Happy birthday, my little sister!" Mia exclaimed, quickly placing her coffee on the side table adorned with exquisite pink orchids, which added a pop of colour to the otherwise muted décor.

Mia was dressed in matching pink silk shorts and a pink top, her toenails polished to perfection. Her natural beauty was accentuated by her clean, manicured nails, plumped lips, and perfectly shaped brows that framed her round face. Long black hair cascaded over her shoulders, catching the dim light filtering in through the gloomy morning. The room was illuminated only by the grey light outside, but the ambience was enhanced by the warm yellow glow from the stylish lamps scattered throughout the space, creating an inviting yet sophisticated atmosphere. "Siri, turn on the lights," Mia commanded, her voice firm and confident. "Siri, play some music," she added, grabbing her creamy cappuccino and opening her laptop.

The Versace furnishings added an air of luxury to the living room, each piece thoughtfully chosen to complement the overall aesthetic. "What's the plan for today?" Mia asked, taking a sip of her coffee, her eyes sparkling with curiosity. "Plan? There are no plans. If this were India, sure, we'd have a huge party lined up. But here? I only know, like, four people," Kavya replied, moving to the coffee machine to prepare herself a cappuccino. "You want a party? I can arrange that for you. Who knows, you might even meet someone special!" Mia suggested, a playful smile dancing on her lips. "Where is this coming from? Who's here to find love?" Kavya rolled her eyes, exasperated. "This is New York, darling! Women come here to find love," Mia said, tilting her head and giving Kavya a teasing look. Kavya laughed, shaking her head. "Really, sister? Sitting in a penthouse on the 88th floor in New York City, you're telling me this? Why would I need a man?" Sarcasm dripped from her words. "Love, my darling. You need a man for emotional support," Mia replied, raising an eyebrow.

"What kind of emotional support? My mom just delivered me a BMW, I love myself, and my trusty dildo does an amazing job! So where does this 'man' stuff come from?" Kavya shot back; her annoyance evident. "You know, when love knocks on your door, all that arrogance will fade away. You'll do anything to keep that man in your life. I could write it down for you," Mia said with a playful grin.

"Men can serve me, and that's enough. Let's just throw a party and have fun! Invite whoever. Besides, you don't even believe in love!" Kavya sank into a chair with her cappuccino, exhaling dramatically. Mia chuckled, knowing Kavya's stubbornness too well. "Let's just move on to the next conversation; it's your birthday!" Kavya rolled her eyes again. "Yes, sure." "All right, I'll post on Facebook," Mia said, pulling out her phone and typing away. "Thank you, my PLASTIC SURGEON sister! And hopefully, you'll find a man tonight!" Kavya teased, reaching over to tickle her. "Dude, I'd love to snuggle up with a man after work, but I never have time to go on a date. The life of a plastic surgeon isn't easy." Mia replied, her fingers flying over the touchscreen as she posted the announcement. Kavya couldn't help but smile at her sister's playful spirit.

Kavya's Birthday Party Invite!

Party Announcement

Hi everyone, we're excited to announce a party! The dress code is formal and casual, and food and drinks will be provided. The party kicks off at 7:00 pm. Please check in at the front desk and mention my name. Feel free to bring a guest along. If you plan to use the hot tub, don't forget to bring your bathing suit! Make sure to arrange your ride home or have a designated driver. Looking forward to seeing you all tonight at our penthouse on the 88th floor. Hope everyone is ready to celebrate!

Posted! "All set, sister! The post is up! Just be ready to shine tonight," Mia said with a satisfied smile.

Kavya quickly checked her phone and reposted the announcement she was tagged in, adding a smiley face to the end. "Man, this sounds like a teenage party! I mean, you're a PLASTIC SURGEON. Who's going to show up without a designated driver?" Kavya scrolled through the comments, raising an eyebrow. "You might be surprised. Plus, growing up is overrated," Mia replied, grabbing her phone to make a call. "Hello, can we please have balloon decoration number 13 from the catalogue for tonight?" Mia requested; her tone professional.

"Ma'am, that's short notice. We usually require a week for advance bookings," came the voice on the other end. "We can pay whatever the cost is for the service. Just make it happen," Mia replied firmly. "Sure, ma'am. We'll need to have more people for this. Please send the address, and we'll require half of the payment in advance. I'll email you the bill; payment can be made online," the voice said.

"Understood," Mia said, hanging up and making a few more calls to food vendors and the bartender. Kavya checked her phone and noticed she had 92 missed calls. Her Instagram, with its million followers, was flooded with birthday messages.

She smiled, grateful for the attention. Just then, the front door swung open, and a woman walked in. Dressed in black pants and a crisp white shirt, her blonde hair was neatly tucked into a bun, and her red lipstick complemented her fair complexion. She was a slender Caucasian woman. "Oh, hello, Maria! How are you?" Mia greeted her warmly. "I'm doing well, Mia. I just wanted to sneak in a smoke before I start cleaning if that's okay?" Maria, the housekeeper, asked. "Of course, my love," Mia replied, still focused on her laptop while taking another call. "It's Kavya's birthday today, Maria! We're having a party," Mia added, multitasking as she made arrangements.

"Happy birthday, Kavya! Do you have a dress for tonight?" Maria inquired. "Thank you, Maria! Oh, right, I need to go shopping! Thanks for the reminder and the birthday wishes," Kavya smiled, appreciating the thoughtfulness. "You better hurry up; it's New York City!" Maria warned playfully. Kavya chuckled. She had been in New York for a while now, and her days often revolved around shopping and exploring the city. Today, she would embrace her birthday in style!

In the Evening

A wooden piano sat forlornly next to the tall building, its keys untouched as the sun set over New York City, painting the sky in shades of pink. Inside the penthouse, the atmosphere buzzed with anticipation as Mia prepared for Kavya's birthday party. The elegant living room that had looked so pristine just hours earlier was now transformed into a vibrant nightclub with flashing lights and a dim ambience.

A beautifully arranged charcuterie board adorned the kitchen counter, enticing guests with its colourful selection. The doorbell chimed, breaking the lively atmosphere. Mia swiftly opened the door to greet her guest. "Oh, hello, Jennifer! How are you?" Mia beamed as a tall blonde woman stepped inside, dressed in a crisp white shirt and tailored black trousers.

"I'm doing very well, Mia. Thank you for inviting me to another one of your fabulous parties!" Jennifer replied, making her way to the bar. With her minimal makeup and effortlessly styled hair down, she exuded a natural beauty. "Of course! You're such an amazing bartender. Why wouldn't I invite you? You've served at nearly 17 of my house parties in the last three months!" Mia exclaimed, standing next to the bar in a fitted black bodycon dress, her gold necklace spelling out her name.

The pink Hermès bracelet on her wrist perfectly complemented her Chanel earrings. "Have you found a boyfriend yet, Mia?" Jennifer asked, organising the glasses behind the bar. "Oh, darling, who has time for that? I own a penthouse in downtown New York. Who needs emotional attachments when a good dildo does the job perfectly?" Mia laughed, taking a sip of the champagne Jennifer poured for her.

Their laughter filled the open living room, setting a light-hearted tone for the evening. The doorbell rang again, and Mia unlocked it with her phone. "Hello! I'm Logan Wilson, your DJ for the night," announced a man dressed in a striking pink cocktail dress. "Oh, hi Logan! It's great to see you again. That dress looks fabulous on you!" Mia responded, handing him a glass of champagne.

A black and gold balloon decoration by the entrance proclaimed, *Happy Birthday, Kavya.* "Thank you, my love! I adore this décor. Where's the birthday girl?" Logan asked, taking his drink and heading over to his DJ setup. "She should be down any minute, and our guests will start arriving soon," Mia replied as Kavya made her way down the stairs. Kavya descended in a stunning long white dress, the sound of her blue satin, jewel buckle, and Manolo Blahnik heels echoing in the room.

She accessorised her look with gold bangles, her hair styled in an elegant bun, and gold earrings glimmering in the light. "Oh, there she is! You look absolutely gorgeous in that white dress!" Mia exclaimed, handing Kavya a champagne glass. The room was alive with light and music, the dance floor glowing invitingly. Both Logan and Jennifer offered their birthday wishes, and Kavya smiled, though a flicker of confusion crossed her face. She leaned towards Mia and whispered, "Why is that man dressed in a dress and wearing makeup? He has chest hair and hairy armpits. Was this a costume party, Mia?" Mia smiled knowingly.

She had seen transgender individuals in Mumbai before, where they were often treated differently, but in New York, anything was possible. "Logan is a good friend of mine. He's transgender; he identifies as a man but loves to dress as a woman. Isn't that a fabulous pink off-shoulder dress?" Mia explained, noticing Kavya's continued confusion. The doorbell rang again, and Mia opened it to welcome more friends.

The night unfolded, and the party began to swell in size. Many of Mia's wealthy friends, who were also her clients, filtered in, leaving Kavya feeling like a stranger among them. Yet, as the birthday girl, she held her head high, champagne glass in hand. A magnificent three-tier cake sat proudly next to the vibrant balloon decorations. "How did you manage to arrange all this in half a day?" Kavya marvelled, taking in the beautifully curated setup. "Not half a day, my dear! The cake was ordered three weeks ago, and the balloon décor was arranged then, too. The DJ is a friend of mine, and with my staff's help, we set everything up amidst my other work commitments," Mia explained, munching on blue cheese and crackers, occasionally tripping over her words.

"Wow, you never cease to amaze me," Kavya said, stealing a cracker from Mia's plate and popping it into her mouth. "Thank you! Now go enjoy the party. The dance floor is lit!" Mia encouraged, fixing a stray hair on Kavya's head.

Keep Doing What You Are Doing!

The ceiling lights illuminated the living room, casting a vibrant glow throughout the penthouse. February in New York was cold, but inside, the chill was forgotten as the space transformed into a lively nightclub atmosphere, complete with pulsating music and colourful lights. The patio featured a smoke show, adding an air of excitement to the festivities.

Kavya never imagined her birthday party would attract 50 to 60 guests. Feeling adventurous, she decided to shed her dress and join the crowd in the hot tub. The patio was adorned with a plush, deep-set sectional sofa, perfectly complementing the hot tub, while a built-in fireplace radiated warmth into the open space.

A bar on the patio drew a line of eager guests, and Mia, a master of hosting, moved seamlessly among them, ensuring everyone was entertained. Kavya navigated through the throngs of partygoers. It was her birthday, yet she felt a sense of freedom in anonymity; no one knew her, allowing her to be herself in a sea of unfamiliar faces. With a Sex-on-the-Beach martini in hand—her seventh or eighth of the night—she wobbled slightly, the sound of her heels drowned out by the booming music.

The well-dressed men and stunning women around her seemed to have stepped out of a glossy magazine, a reflection of Mia's talent for attracting an aesthetically pleasing crowd. Stepping outside to the patio bar, Kavya placed her empty glass on a stone table, scanning the lively scene. The couches were filled with laughter and conversation, the atmosphere warm and inviting.

"Hey birthday girl! Jump in the hot tub with us!" someone called out. Kavya turned to see the source of the voice. As she approached, she noticed a man lounging in the hot tub, clad in shorts. "Hello," she greeted him, curiosity piqued. "Want to join us?" the Caucasian man asked, his tone friendly. Kavya hesitated.

"I think I might pass," she replied, aware that she had no bathing suit underneath her dress and feeling a bit self-conscious about her makeup. "Come on! It's all in good fun! I'm Matt, by the way!" he said, extending his hand towards her. "Nice to meet you, Matt." Kavya shook his hand, her eyes drifting over his well-built physique. He appeared to be in his late thirties, with a tattoo on his triceps and impressive abs visible even as he sat. She found him undeniably attractive.

"I'm Jonathan," another man chimed in, waving from the tub. He looked to be in his mid-thirties, exuding a relaxed charm. "Hey, gorgeous! I'm Nikki! Happy birthday, darling!" a blonde woman greeted her, her long nails and plump lips accentuating her beauty. Her hair was styled in a bun, and her form-fitting outfit highlighted her toned figure. Kavya took a sip of her beer and set it down on the wooden deck near the tub. With a burst of confidence, she decided to join the fun.

She slipped off her dress, hanging it on a nearby hook, revealing her red bra and panties. Navigating her way to the hot tub, Kavya stumbled slightly, laughter bubbling up as she tried to maintain her balance. Matt offered her his arm, and she gratefully latched onto him as they made their way into the bubbling water alongside four others. "It's a great party!" Matt remarked, glancing over at Kavya. "Mia deserves all the credit," she replied, retrieving her drink from the edge of the tub.

"Cheers!" Matt clinked his beer can against hers, his eyes sparkling with interest. Jonathan, Nikki, Scott, and Kourtney joined in, raising their glasses in a toast. "How do you know my cousin?" Kavya asked, intrigued. "Well, she's my plastic surgeon," Matt replied, a grin on his face. "Oh, what? Did you get those six-pack abs implanted?" Kavya laughed, enjoying the banter. "Very funny! I'm actually a firefighter and had some burns," he said, smiling back. "That's cool! But I think I'm done in the tub for now. I'm going to get changed," Kavya stood up, slightly unsteady, but Matt offered her support as he rose to his feet as well. "I'm about done too. Could you grab me a towel? I forgot mine," he asked, towering over her at 6'2". "Sure! Follow me," she said, leading him through the crowd and up the stairs. In a whirlwind of hospitality and perhaps a touch of inebriation, she ushered him into her bedroom to get a towel. The floor was slick with the water dripping from Kavya's bra and panties.

"It's a beautiful room," Matt commented, taking in the elegant décor. Kavya opened her closet, retrieved a towel, and handed it to him. As he wiped himself off, she noticed her own bra and panties had slipped to the floor.

In an unexpected turn of events, the mundane task of fetching a towel took a risqué detour. Before they knew it, the birthday suit became the only attire on Kavya's agenda. Kavya stood beside Matt, feeling the heat radiating from him. They both jumped onto the bed, laughter turning into something more intimate. "Oh God, you are so hot," Kavya breathed as they found themselves naked on her bed. Matt kissed her neck, holding her tightly as Kavya rode him, lost in the moment.

He pulled her closer, they moved together in a rhythm that felt intoxicating. Matt's lips found her breasts, and Kavya felt herself melt under his touch. The water from the hot tub had dried off, replaced by the heat of their bodies. Just as Kavya was about to get lost in her thoughts, Matt sank his face between her legs.

"Oh God, dear Lord! Jonathan, you are amazing!" she moaned, gripping the pillows tightly. "Jonathan? I'm Matt," he reminded her, pulling back in surprise. Kavya, ever the pragmatic problem-solver, smirked and said, "Can you just keep going and we can sort out the names later?"

"As you wish," Matt replied with a playful grin, diving back into the moment. Kavya surrendered to pleasure as he pulled her legs to the edge of the bed, holding them on his shoulders while moving inside her. She closed her eyes, lost in the sensations, her body responding to his every touch. Half an hour slipped away in a haze of passion, and they lay entwined, breathing heavily as the sounds of the party echoed in the background.

Matt eventually pulled on his shorts and stood up, glancing back at Kavya. "I'll see you downstairs?" he asked with a smile. She nodded, still reeling from the whirlwind of events. As he walked out, she couldn't help but reflect on the extraordinary encounter they had shared, even if it had happened so quickly. Kavya rolled back into her bed, pulling the blanket around her and feeling her legs still shaking from the intensity of their connection. The evening had unfolded into a whimsical blend of spontaneity and excitement, a curious anecdote that would surely be shared among the partygoers for years to come.

The Red Bubble

In the bustling backstage of a glamorous fashion show in the heart of New York City, Kavya found herself in a whirlwind of activity. Surrounded by the talented Sarah and an African makeup artist, she sat patiently as they delicately applied layers of black-and-white makeup to her face, transforming her into a work of art. Amidst the chaos, her phone suddenly came to life with a soft vibration. With a graceful motion, Kavya reached out to grab the device, her eyes flickering with curiosity. As she attempted to use the phone's face recognition feature, a slight frown creased her brow. The intricate makeup obscured her natural features, causing the device to fail to recognise her. Undeterred, Kavya glanced around the room and noticed a striking mural adorning the wall, featuring a mysterious motor as its centrepiece. With a hint of determination in her gaze, she decided to take matters into her own hands. With a swift movement, she began to manually enter the password, each tap of her fingers a testament to her resourcefulness and adaptability in the face of unexpected challenges.

"Kavya, concentrate," came the voice, pulling her attention back to the present. She sat nervously in a chair, receiving her finishing touches before stepping onto the runway that evening for a local designer in New York City. "Don't move a muscle! You could ruin everything," the chaos of the backstage enveloped her, filled with models, hairstylists, and makeup artists, all hurriedly preparing for the show. There was no room for error here. "You're a blank canvas for the makeup artist," Sarah, a makeup artist with a warm smile, said as she deftly inserted mousse into Kavya's hair, styling it into perfect loops on her forehead. If she were in India, Kavya thought, she would have her own dedicated makeup artist and van, just like her father, a well-known actor. But here, in New York City, she was just another face in the crowd—ordinary, with her assigned number 12. Americans struggled to pronounce her name, opting for "Ka-Vi-Ya." Life felt a bit unjust at the moment. But whoever claimed life was easy? It was a common misconception that being the child of a celebrity meant a life without challenges. Sure, there were perks, but much of it was merely a facade, masking the complexities beneath. Kavya's thoughts drifted to

India, where the sunsets and sunrises were truly priceless, especially in Mumbai—the city that never slept. This city was always aglow, but it was not Mumbai; it was New York—the bustling metropolis—on a Wednesday evening in March. Life here might not be fair, but it was undeniably liberating. A red notification bubble flashed in her mind, teasing her with its presence. She hesitated to open it, fearing the unknown it might reveal—like a warning sign. Why was red always associated with alerts? Why not a softer hue? Red screamed danger, fire, and urgency. She focused intently on her reflection in the mirror. "Oh boy," Kavya exhaled deeply. Despite the ominous message, there was a silver lining—she could choose to ignore it for now. The little notification could wait, but curiosity lingered. It was likely from Matt. She was not the best at face-to-face conversations with him. Her mind raced like a sports car. What would he say? She couldn't even recall his name.

Gazing into the mirror, she saw a dark, gothic version of herself, adorned in a dress made entirely of balloons. "Yes, Jonathan," she mused, almost dreamily. "I'm not Jonathan. I'm Matt," a voice interrupted. "Oh, you're not? Well, just keep doing what you're doing for now. We can sort this out later," she remembered saying, her memories of the previous night hazy from too much alcohol. Kavya scratched her head, still feeling the effects of last night's celebration. The hangover was a lingering reminder of her birthday bash.

"NUMBER 12, RUN!" a voice called, snapping her back to reality. She stood up and made her way to the runway for South India New York Fashion Week. As she stepped onto the runway, the brilliance of the lights was blinding, yet familiar. The flashes of cameras were something she was accustomed to, being the daughter of a famous actor. Kavya walked confidently, though fragments of last night's party replayed in her mind. She was so inebriated that she couldn't remember who she'd woken up next to. How embarrassing! The bright lights illuminated her as she approached the media pit. The balloon dress she wore crunched with each step, a sound lost beneath the pulsating music that drowned out all other noise. At this moment, she felt invisible, despite the spotlight on her. Everyone knew she was a celebrity's daughter, but on this runway, she was just Kavya, number 12, longing to escape the clutches of this extravagant life.

Once her turn on the runway concluded, she hurried back to the backstage area, relieved to shed the balloon dress. "Well done, darling! You were fantastic!" Mia, her friend, applauded, giving Kavya a quick kiss on the cheek. "Let's grab something to eat," Mia suggested as they exited the venue, still bustling with energy. "Shall we stroll through Central Park, or would a cab be better?" Mia asked as they walked along the street. "I think a cab is wise, especially with this gothic makeup," Kavya chuckled. "Sounds good to me! Who wouldn't want to flaunt gothic glam?" Mia replied, pulling out her phone to order an Uber.

A Tesla SUV pulled up, and they climbed in. "Please take us to the restaurant, Shubham," Mia instructed the driver, a man in his mid-40s dressed casually. Kavya scrolled through her phone while Mia chatted away. The atmosphere was oddly quiet; three people in an Uber, yet no one spoke. The red notification bubble still loomed on her screen. Despite its presence, she had no intention of opening it. She felt no guilt about what had happened, but she couldn't shake the feeling of embarrassment for forgetting the guy's name. What would he think of her, sitting in an Uber with her dramatic makeup? Kavya shook her head. It didn't matter; they likely wouldn't cross paths again. But that red bubble nagged at her. Finally, she summoned the courage to click on it. The message was from Matt. "Hey, baby girl. Last night was incredible. Want to meet up for dinner this Friday?" Kavya groaned in annoyance, shaking her head. "What's wrong, Kav?" Mia noticed her reaction. With her eyes heavily made up and her lips dark, Kavya rolled her eyes in frustration. "Tell me what's up?" Mia pressed. Kavya remained silent, nodding her head towards the South Asian Uber driver, who was oblivious to their conversation. The silence thickened, a mystery hanging in the air that Mia was eager to unravel. Half an hour later, they arrived at the restaurant. "I slept with this guy, and I can't remember his name. Now he's asking me out for dinner," Kavya confessed, showing Mia the message that had just popped up. "That's it? That's what's bothering you? If you like him, go for dinner! If it was just a fling, tell him so," Mia, a plastic surgeon, advised. "Well, it was just a one-night stand. I doubt he's boyfriend material—some guys are just for fun," Kavya replied, tucking her phone back into her purse. Mia laughed. "We've arrived! Let's grab a table. I need all the details." As they stood in line, Kavya couldn't shake the feeling that her life was about to take another unexpected turn.

The Chef

“Good evening,” greeted a tall Caucasian man in a tailored black suit as he opened the door. You would think that by 2024, restaurants would have adopted sliding doors, but this place was old-school, opting for charm over modern convenience.

Perhaps it was a classy choice, or maybe just a reminder of how technology could replace jobs. “Oh wow, a handsome doorman,” Kavya remarked as she stepped inside, exhaling a deep sigh.

“Are you drooling?” Mia teased as they found themselves in the nearly empty lobby, the music pulsing through the air. “I am not drooling! Seriously, who drools over a doorman?” Kavya rolled her eyes dramatically.

"With that dark makeup on? Good luck charming even a doorman," Mia laughed as they approached the reception desk. "Good evening! Welcome to Per Se. May I have your name, please?" asked a tall blonde in a sleek black dress, her hair cascading down.

"Hi there! It's Mia, for two, please." The receptionist grabbed a menu and led them to a cosy table by the window, where they could admire the twinkling lights of the city. "Your server will be with you shortly. Enjoy your menu," she said, placing it on the table before disappearing. The atmosphere was warm, filled with the hum of conversations, the clatter of cutlery, and the upbeat music. Just the two of them at the table, they settled in. "So, what happened?" Mia leaned in, her curiosity piqued. "What do you mean?" Kavya replied, feigning surprise. "You know exactly what I'm talking about—the guy!" Mia urged, her makeup-free face glowing in the soft lights, her outfit hugging her toned figure perfectly. "Oh, that. His name is Matt, not Jonathan. We just had a casual night. He was drinking, and I was so drunk I couldn't even remember his name. Not that I was looking to marry him," Kavya explained, scrolling through her phone to show Mia. "Oh, dinner date? Matt is my personal trainer—quite the charmer," Mia winked as she perused the menu.

"Blocked. Let's just focus on the food. What are you getting?" Kavya set her phone down, her mind still swirling. A male server approached their table. "How are you ladies doing this evening?" "It's going great! We just came from her fashion show," Mia pointed at Kavya, who still sported her dramatic black-and-white makeup. "Oh, that's amazing! I was wondering what the makeup was for," the server said, glancing at Kavya with interest. "It's not just the makeup; the dress was wild too—made entirely of balloons!" Kavya added, noticing the look of confusion on his face.

"Well, it sounds like you two have had quite the evening. Are you ready to order?" the server asked. "Yes, I'll have the spaghetti carbonara, please," Kavya replied. "I'll go with the Margherita Pizza and a bottle of wine, thank you," Mia added. "Excellent choices! Your orders will be up shortly," the server said with a smile before heading off. After a short wait, their food arrived, the aroma wafting tantalizingly in the air.

The pizza and spaghetti looked divine, just what they needed after a long day. The server poured wine into their glasses and left. "The server looked so confused," Kavya said as she took a bite of her spaghetti, the black lipstick leaving a mark on her glass. Mia chuckled. "Why wouldn't he be confused? Your face is painted black and white!" "Just another night in New York City, sitting here with my painted face, feeling like a total mess," Kavya said, taking a sip of her wine. "Well, feeling like a mess isn't the worst thing. It just means you're hot and can get whoever you want," Mia replied, enjoying her meal. Kavya laughed. "Thanks, cousin. That's exactly the pep talk I needed when a guy is asking me out, and I just want to text him back saying it was a one-time thing." "What's stopping you? Just send it," Mia urged, locking eyes with Kavya. "That would be so rude! Maybe I could just go for coffee instead of dinner?" Kavya suggested. "Please, darling. Stop feeling guilty for having fun. I'm sure guys do the same—hook up and forget!" Mia rolled her eyes. "Hello, ladies. How are you this evening?" A tall man approached their table. Kavya was still processing Mia's words when she caught sight of him.

He stood about 5'8", perhaps in his late 30s, with a well-built frame and a tanned complexion. His combed-over hair was neatly parted, and his biceps were visible under his crisp white dress shirt. Kavya scanned him from head to toe, momentarily speechless. "The evening is going wonderfully, and the food is absolutely delicious," Mia exclaimed, her enthusiasm contrasting with Kavya's quiet awe. "I'm glad to hear that. My name is Kiaan, and I'm the chef here, just checking in on your experience," he said, hands clasped in front of him, his smile radiant. "It truly is a lovely evening. Thank you," Mia responded, while Kavya remained captivated, her gaze locked on Kiaan.

"I'll let you enjoy your meal. I'll send over a complimentary dessert for you two. Have a wonderful evening," Kiaan said before moving on to the next table. "Back to the Matt/Jonathan situation—are you going to reply?" Mia asked, but Kavya was still entranced by the chef's presence. "I told you, I blocked him, Mia. Can we please talk about something else?" Kavya discreetly sipped her wine, using the glass as a shield while stealing glances at Kiaan. Her mind was racing, completely absorbed in thoughts of him, and she struggled to focus on anything Mia was saying. Could she confide in Mia about her sudden attraction to the chef? Probably not, especially when their conversation was still fixated on her one-night stand.

Mansion in My Head

The soft chime of the doorbell announced Kavya and Mia's arrival at the Hermès boutique. The scent of luxury wafted through the air, mingling with the faint aroma of freshly brewed coffee from a nearby café. Kavya felt a thrill of excitement as she stepped inside, her eyes sparkling with anticipation. She had been looking forward to this shopping trip, not just for the exquisite pieces that Hermès offered, but for a chance to share her newfound crush with her best friend.

"Okay, spill it!" Mia said, her voice a mix of curiosity and mischief as they browsed through the displays of elegant scarves and handbags.

"What's got you so giddy today? You've been floating on a cloud ever since you saw that chef."

Kavya blushed, her cheeks turning a delicate shade of pink. "It's just... I don't know, Mia. There's something about him. I only saw him once, but he was so passionate while he was greeting us. His focus, the way he… Mia—ugh, it was mesmerising! It has been a few weeks or months now but he has a mansion in my head."

Mia raised an eyebrow, a teasing smile creeping onto her face. "You're in serious trouble, girl. We were supposed to get you a job, not a man," she laughed.

Kavya playfully swatted her arm. "Right job. Maybe I can get a job in his restaurant."

"Girl, slow down. Do you even remember his name? Also, your face was all painted when we had a in these," Mia asked, glancing at a display of bags. "Or are we going to refer to him as 'the mysterious chef' for the rest of eternity? Plus, he didn't even see you. Your face was painted black and white."

"You already forgot his name? Kiaan. He was talking to you," Kavya said, her voice bubbling with excitement. "Oh right. He didn't see me. Even better. I can get a job as a waitress."

Mia's eyes sparkled with mischief. "Oh no, this sounds like a recipe for disaster. You're going to swoop in like a lovebird and make a fool of yourself, aren't you?"

Kavya rolled her eyes but couldn't suppress her grin. "Maybe. But wouldn't it be worth it? I mean, what if he's as amazing as I think he is? What if he makes the best risotto in the city?"

"Or is he the complete opposite of what you are thinking? Maybe he is just a player and a cokehead?" Mia shot back, trying to keep a straight face.

"You really should consider all possibilities before you fall head over heels," Mia suggests.

Kavya sighed dramatically, leaning against a nearby shelf. "I know, I know. But I just can't help it. When I saw him, it felt like everything clicked. I've never felt this way about someone before."

Mia tilted her head, her expression softening. "That's sweet, Kavya. But you also need to be careful. Love at first sight can be misleading. What if he turns out to be a total jerk? You are my little sister. I am just warning you."

"Then I'll just have to drown my sorrows in designer handbags," Kavya replied, her eyes twinkling.

"Speaking of which, check this out!" She picked up a stunning silk scarf, its intricate patterns swirling with vibrant colours. "Isn't this gorgeous?" Mia's eyes widened, and she took the scarf from Kavya's hands, admiring it.

"It is gorgeous, darling. Just buy it. Really, who needs a man when you have a wallet full of cash?" Mia takes the bag and places it against her body.

“Plus I might not ever get him, but I will always have this, baby,” Mia takes the purse from her and presses it against her body.

“So, what’s your game plan? Just walk in and say, ‘Hey, I’m Kavya, and I’m in love with you because you make a mean carbonara?’” Kavya burst out laughing, the sound echoing through the upscale shopping district. “That’s more like you. You would do that to a man,” Kavya laughs.

“I would totally do that to a man if I was in love or if someone challenged me. But who has time for a man?” Mia said, smirking.

Kavya approached the sales associate with a gleam in her eye, pointing to a stunning handbag on display. Kavya said, “Hi! I absolutely love this bag. What can you tell me about it?”

Sales associate: “Good afternoon! This is our smooth calfskin leather handbag with gold-tone hardware. It features a turn-lock closure and comes with a spacious main compartment. It’s priced at $45,000.”

Kavya holds onto the bag, “I absolutely love this baby pink. Let’s buy it. What do you think, Mia?”

“You love it? Then buy it,” Mia agrees.

The sales associate stands there while Kavya looks at the bag. "Absolutely. Hermès bags are timeless pieces that hold their value. Plus, the craftsmanship is exceptional."

"Sold. Let's pay," Kavya walks with Mia and follows the salesperson to the counter. She walks out of the store with a smile.

"Oh, looks like you love your purse more than a man," Mia jokes.

"I will always love a Birkin bag more than any man," they both laugh.

Gift Card

Kavya lay sprawled across her plush bed, scrolling through her Instagram feed. She had just posted a vibrant photo dump of her adventures from April and May, and the likes were pouring in—30,000 and counting. She smiled, basking in the virtual adoration, but her mind kept drifting back to one particular face: Kiaan, the charming chef she had spotted at the restaurant two months ago.

"The only heart that I want is that man's heart in the restaurant," she whispered, placing her phone on her nightstand. She stared at the ceiling, lost in her thoughts, until suddenly, an idea sparked in her mind. With renewed energy, she jumped out of bed.

Picking up her phone, she dialled Lush Nail Lounge, her go-to salon. "Hello, Lush Lounge. Madeline speaking. How may I help you?" came the cheerful voice. "Hi, Madeline! It's Kavya. Can I make an appointment for today?" she asked, her tone urgent.

"Hello, Kavya. I'm fully booked for today. I can schedule you for tomorrow," Madeline replied, her tone polite but firm. Kavya felt a wave of frustration.

"Actually, I need my nails redone today. Can you squeeze me in?" Madeline paused, "I'm sorry, but there are no cancellations. I can't fit you in today."

Kavya's mind raced. "Madeline, it's really important. What if I covered your clients' charges and mine as well?" "I can't do that," Madeline said gently. "I've already made commitments."

"Okay, thank you," Kavya said, her heart sinking as she hung up the phone. Thoughts of Kiaan swirled in her head. How could she ask him out? She was used to getting what she wanted, but this was different. Kavya began pacing her room, her mind racing. What if she worked at the restaurant? It would be the perfect way to get close to Kiaan.

Sure, she had no experience, but love could make one do anything. "Forget about experience," she muttered to herself. She had never even lifted a dish in her life—she had a full kitchen staff at her disposal.

But if she became a waitress, she would have to remove her long, glamorous nails. She glanced at her perfectly manicured fingers. "How do you pull your pants up with these nails?" she mused, imagining herself in a waitress uniform instead of her usual designer dresses. Kiaan had taken up residence in her mind, occupying every corner with thoughts of their possible future.

She envisioned him sweeping her off her feet, carrying her to his bed, and showering her with kisses. "What is life without love?" Kavya sighed, shaking her head at her own daydreams. There was no time to waste. With newfound determination, she slipped into her jacket and headed for the door.

"Hello, Doorman," she said absently to Liam, the doorman, who held the door open for her. She hopped into her BMW and drove to Lush Nail Lounge, parking outside the elegant salon. As she walked in, the air smelled of fresh polish and sweet scents, with upbeat music playing in the background. Happy women chatted and laughed, indulging in luxurious treatments.

Kavya spotted Madeline, who was busy at her station, working on a client's nails. She approached Madeline's desk with purpose. "Oh, hello, Kavya! You're here," Madeline said, a hint of surprise in her voice.

"Hi, Maddy. I need these nails off, please," Kavya said, extending her hand. Madeline glanced at the blonde woman in the chair next to her, who looked at Kavya with wide eyes.

"I told you I have a client," Madeline replied, pointing at the woman. "But since I'm here, can't you get me someone else?" Kavya asked, desperation creeping into her voice. Suddenly, she pulled out a crisp $200 bill from her purse. "Ma'am," she said, bending slightly to make eye contact with the blonde.

"I really need these nails off today. I can offer you £200 or more to give up this appointment. It's really important."

The blonde woman, still looking confused, glanced between Kavya and Madeline. Kavya took out another £100 note and added it to the first. "Okay, please take £300," she insisted, holding out the cash. After a moment of awkward silence, the blonde reached out and took the money.

"Fine. I'll take £300. You can have this appointment," she said, standing up and walking away. Madeline shook her head, laughter spilling from her lips. "You are a crazy rich Indian!" she said, guiding Kavya to a chair.

Kavya grinned sheepishly as Madeline began to soak her acrylics in a solution. "I know it's a bit much, but I really need these nails gone," she replied.

"I just did these for you four days ago! What happened?" Madeline asked, her curiosity piqued. Kavya looked at her hands, then back at Madeline.

"Well, Maddy, I'm applying for a job and I don't need nails for that." "Oh, that's great news! Where are you applying?" Madeline asked, wrapping aluminium foil around Kavya's fingers to speed up the removal process.

"It's at a restaurant as a waitress," Kavya said, her voice filled with excitement. Madeline raised an eyebrow, clearly puzzled. "A waitress? That's nice, but it seems a bit out of character for you."

Kavya smiled, understanding Madeline's confusion. "Maddy, I'm in love with the chef," she confessed, her cheeks flushing slightly. "Oh, now I see why you're applying for the waitress job," Madeline said, relief washing over her features. "You really like this guy!" Kavya nodded, laughter bubbling up.

"I spill all my beans to you. You're a great secret keeper." As the music pulsed in the background, the two women shared a moment of understanding, the salon buzzing with laughter and chatter around them.

Dated Retail!

Kavya stood in front of her expansive walk-in closet, a flurry of emotions swirling inside her. Today was the day she would drop off her resume at the restaurant, and she was determined to make the right impression. As she paced back and forth, her eyes scanned the rows of designer clothing that hung elegantly before her. "What should I wear?" she murmured to herself, pulling out a stunning designer dress, only to quickly dismiss it.

"No, that's not right. I need to look like a waitress, not a celebrity." The thought of walking into the restaurant in her usual luxury attire made her cringe. To convince the manager to give her a chance, she needed to blend in rather than stand out. After several minutes of searching, she finally settled on a simple white button-up shirt and a pair of well-fitted jeans. "This will do," she said with determination, slipping into the outfit.

It felt comfortable yet polished, perfect for her mission. As she looked at herself in the mirror, she felt a mix of excitement and anxiety. Butterflies danced in her stomach at the thought of Kiaan, the handsome chef who had captivated her with just one glance.

"Okay, let's do this," she said, taking a deep breath before heading downstairs. When she reached the building's front door, she spotted Liam, the doorman. "Doorman, can you please bring my car?" she asked, handing him her keys. He nodded silently, taking her keys and heading outside to fetch her BMW.

"Here you go, madam," Liam said as he returned, handing her the keys with a polite smile. Kavya hopped into her car and merged into the busy streets of New York. However, as she sat in traffic, she suddenly realised that driving her luxury SUV to a waitress job didn't quite fit the occasion.

"Ah, what was I thinking?" she exclaimed, tapping her forehead in frustration. Quickly, she turned the car into a nearby parking lot and called a taxi instead.

The drive to the restaurant should have taken about 40 minutes, but with the taxi, it felt like an eternity. Kavya's mind raced with thoughts of how to convince the manager to hire her. What would she say? "Ma'am, we're here," the cab driver announced, breaking her from her thoughts.

She looked out of the window, spotting the restaurant's elegant facade. "Thank you," she replied, tapping her card to pay the fare before stepping out of the taxi. Taking a deep breath, she gathered her resume and headed towards the entrance, her heart pounding with anticipation. As she entered, the doorman held the door open for her, and she was greeted by a blonde receptionist.

"Good morning! How can I help you?" the receptionist asked with a friendly smile. "Can I please see the manager?" Kavya's eyes scanned the restaurant, searching for Kiaan. Just the thought of him made her heart race. "Sure, please have a seat, and I'll have him come over," the receptionist replied.

Kavya nodded and took a seat on a plush leather couch, feeling the nerves bubble up inside her. It wasn't the job that made her anxious; it was the thought of being near Kiaan. Before long, a man in a navy blue suit approached her.

"Hello, how can I help you?" he asked, his voice professional yet warm. Kavya stood up, handing him her resume. "Hello, I was wondering if there were any vacancies." "Oh, you're applying for a waitress job?"

he asked, glancing at her resume. She nodded, her heart racing.

"Well, we're not hiring for that position right now," he said, handing back her resume. Kavya felt her heart sink. "I'll take any job. It would be a real honour to work at such a prestigious restaurant," she pleaded, willing to do anything to be closer to Kiaan. "I understand, but we don't have an opening. Sorry," he replied, turning to walk away.

Panic surged through Kavya. She had to think fast. "Wait!" she called out, stopping him in his tracks. "I used to work in retail, and I'm willing to do anything. I'll clean dishes, help in the kitchen—whatever it takes. Let's just say I was dating my retail job, and now I want to get married to the restaurant job," she added with a hopeful smile.

The manager chuckled, clearly amused. "That's a funny way to put it. Let's go have a chat in my office," he said, taking her resume again. Kavya followed him through the restaurant, her eyes scanning the area in hopes of catching a glimpse of Kiaan.

Just as they passed the kitchen, she caught a fleeting glimpse of him. Her heart fluttered, but they continued walking. "Please have a seat," the manager said, gesturing for her to sit in a green leather chair in front of his oak desk. Kavya took a moment to observe the office, which was adorned with awards and framed accolades.

She felt a mix of nervousness and excitement as the man settled in front of her. "So, let's start with your name. It says 'Kav' on your resume," he prompted. "Yes, Kav is short for Kavya," she replied, offering a warm smile. "Tell me about yourself and why you want to work here. I see you worked in retail for six months. What did you do before that?" he asked, his expression curious.

Kavya's mind raced as she prepared her response. She knew she would have to weave a few fabrications to land this job, but her feelings for Kiaan pushed her forward. "I'm from India and arrived in New York about six months ago. I worked in a retail store, but I feel that the hospitality industry is where I truly belong. It's fascinating to me," she said, crafting her story as she spoke.

"Just six months ago? May I ask what you did back in India?" he inquired, his interest piqued. "I worked in a call centre," Kavya replied, a hint of hesitation creeping into her voice as she navigated through her lies. "Well, Kav," he began, leaning against his desk, "we're not hiring a waitress at the moment, but we could use some extra hands in the kitchen since Christmas is coming up. Would that interest you?"

Kavya's eyes lit up with excitement. "Oh yes! I would love to be a kitchen helper!" The thought of being close to Kiaan sent a thrill through her. "Then you have a job," he said with a smile. "You'll need to clean dishes, mop the floor, chop vegetables, and do whatever the chef requests." Kavya nodded eagerly. "When do I start?" "Tomorrow. We open at 11:00 am for breakfast and close at 11:00 pm," he replied, his demeanour friendly.

"Great! I'll see you at 11:00 am tomorrow," Kavya said as she stood up, a mix of excitement and nerves swirling within her. As she walked out of the restaurant, she couldn't shake the feeling of hope. She was determined to find a way to win over Kiaan, even if it meant starting from the bottom. Little did she know, this leap of faith was only the beginning of her journey towards love.

Never Go Crazy Over a Dude!

Kavya slipped into the backseat of the taxi, her heart racing with a mix of excitement and nerves. She had just landed a job as a kitchen helper, and thoughts of Kiaan—the man she had fallen for at first sight—swirled in her mind. Love at first sight was a rare thing, but she felt it deeply. The digital age, however, has complicated the pursuit of romance.

With determination, she pulled out her phone and searched for Kiaan. Her fingers danced across the screen until she found the restaurant's Instagram page. It boasted 11.3k followers. Kavya couldn't help but compare; she had 2.3 million followers.

She shook her head, wondering how something so trivial could matter in the grand scheme of things.

"Ma'am, your stop is here," the driver said, breaking her reverie.

"Oh, thank you!" she replied, glancing out to see she had arrived at Mia's workplace. As she tapped her card to pay, she typed a $150 tip.

"Ma'am, the fare is only £13. I think you accidentally tapped £150 as a tip," the driver said, his dark skin marked with chickenpox scars that gave him an intimidating appearance.

"Oh no, I meant to! I'm just really happy because I got a job!" Kavya beamed, her excitement spilling over. "Congratulations, ma'am. It must be in this building," he said, glancing at the towering structure in the heart of New York City.

"No, it's at a restaurant. I start as a dishwasher tomorrow!" she squealed, clapping her hands together in delight. As she opened the door and stepped out, the driver stared at her with a furrowed brow, tilting his head in bewilderment. He shook his head as he drove off.

"Poor girl. Must be out of her mind—$150 tip for a dishwasher job?" Kavya took the elevator to the 36th floor, her heart still racing with anticipation. The doors opened to a corridor adorned with fresh flower arrangements in golden vases, creating an atmosphere reminiscent of a luxurious hotel lobby. She walked to her left, pushing open a glass door to reach the reception desk. "Can I please see Mia?" she asked the young Asian woman behind the counter, whose name tag read Cheng. "Do you have an appointment?" Cheng inquired, her tone polite yet businesslike.

"No, but please let her know Kavya is here. I'm her cousin," Kavya explained, her eagerness palpable. "Okay, please have a seat. I will inform Dr. Mia that you are here," Cheng said, gesturing towards a plush green velvet couch.

Kavya settled onto the couch, taking in the Ethiopian-inspired décor that filled the room. Just then, Mia appeared in her blue scrubs, looking slightly frazzled but ready to greet her. "Oh hey, Kav! What's going on? Are you okay?" Mia asked, her surprise evident.

"I'm fine! I was just nearby and thought I'd stop by. But it looks like I came at the wrong time," Kavya said, trying to mask her disappointment. "It's always the wrong time here at my clinic. Sorry, I'm really tightly scheduled for another hour. How about you go shopping, and I'll call you when I'm done?" "Oh, that's okay! I'll wait right here. This clinic of yours is just as nice as a five-star hotel lobby."

Kavya assured her, attempting to lift the mood. Mia smiled, her expression softening. "You can tell me all about it once I'm done." An hour passed, filled with the muted sounds of the clinic.

"All right, babe, come on in! It's your turn," Mia called out, her voice brightening. "Wow, that hour went by fast!" Kavya exclaimed, rising from the velvet couch and following Mia into her office. "So, what's going on?"

Mia asked as they both took their seats. "I got a job at the restaurant where we ate after the fashion show," Kavya said, narrowing her eyes and raising an eyebrow, gauging Mia's reaction. "Oh, is that so? And what will you be doing? You would make an excellent receptionist for a starting job in New York," Mia asked, her surprise morphing into concern.

"Kitchen helper," Kavya replied, a hint of uncertainty creeping into her voice.

"A kitchen helper? That means cleaning floors, washing dishes, chopping vegetables, taking out the garbage... and so on. You do realise what you're signing up for, right?" Mia raised an eyebrow, scepticism etched on her face.

"I'm aware of it," Kavya said, though her hesitation was evident.

"You were aware of it," Mia chuckled, shaking her head. "You need some experience or skill for this. This is a joke, right?" Mia questioned in frustration.

"Acting? I can act, right? I can pretend to be a dishwasher and follow instructions—just like in the movies!" Kavya shrugged, trying to defend her choice.

Mia leaned in closer, sitting on the edge of her desk, her frustration evident. "Kav, are you serious? Am I missing something here?"

"I'm in love, Mia, with Kiaan. The chef!" Kavya's voice softened as she confessed, her eyes shifting to the floor before meeting Mia's gaze.

"The chef?" Mia exclaimed, hitting the table with her palm. "You know you can just walk into the restaurant and ask him out, right? You don't have to resort to scrubbing dishes for a man!"

Silence hung heavily between them. "Kav, I'm not speaking French here. How much time are you wasting? It's not that complicated! You saw him for, what, less than a minute when he was at our table?"

Mia adjusted her glasses, looking at Kavya through the lenses. Still, there was silence.

"Look at me. I live off my vibrator most of the time. Who has the energy for a man? You first take off your clothes, then do the work, and then put your clothes back on. And the worst part? You don't even know if you'll get a guaranteed orgasm! And here you are, preparing to work as a kitchen helper. Miss Kavya in the kitchen! Have you ever boiled an egg in your life? Or even picked up a dish? What do I tell your mother?" Mia shook her head in disbelief. Silence lingered once more.

"And what happens when he finds out you have 2.3 million followers on Instagram? You're wealthy, Kavya! You could own the restaurant and have him working for you!" Mia's frustration mounted.

"No, he won't find out. The blue check or followers don't matter anymore. Anyone can buy them and claim they're a public figure or influencer," Kavya insisted, her confidence unwavering.

"Babe, never chase a man. Love should find you; it isn't the other way around. This isn't a rational idea. It's not a cooking class or a culinary school. It's a job—an actual job you've never done before!" Mia exclaimed, her tone firm.

"For love, you do anything. You move mountains!" Kavya shot back, her gaze steady despite Mia's evident frustration. "Okay, great. Go move those mountains. I have to take my next appointment. I'll see you at home after I'm done," Mia said, sitting back in her chair, signalling that their conversation was over. Kavya stood up; her heart heavy yet resolute. As she walked out, Mia slammed the door behind her, the sound echoing in the silence of the clinic.

First Day!

“Hello. What is your name?” Kiaan asked, his voice smooth and commanding as he stood in the bustling kitchen, surrounded by the clatter of pots and pans.

“Kavya,” she replied, her back growing slick with sweat and her mouth suddenly dry. She couldn’t believe she was in the same room as Kiaan, the man who had captured her heart with just one glance. Her heart raced as she took in his presence, the way he moved with confidence and purpose. This was love at first sight, and it left her breathless.

Kiaan was striking, with a neatly trimmed beard that framed a strong jawline. As she glanced closer, she noticed a silver streak of hair at his temple, adding an air of maturity to his youthful demeanour. Peeking beneath his shirt and apron, she caught a glimpse of his well-defined chest, and her breath hitched. His broad shoulders hinted at hours spent working hard, and she felt utterly captivated by him.

"All right. I'm Kiaan, chef and owner of this restaurant," he said, his attention partially on the carrots he was preparing. "You'll need to have your hair tied up before you enter my kitchen." He handed her a handful of carrots, his fingers brushing against hers ever so slightly.

"Once you have your hair up, okay? Wash these carrots and peel them. We start our day with the prep, and you'll be assisting with peeling, cutting, and washing the meat and vegetables. You'll also be responsible for loading and unloading the dishwasher. By the end of your shift, please make sure the floor is cleaned up. Do you understand what I'm saying?" He met her gaze, and she felt a bolt of electricity shoot through her.

Kavya nodded in agreement, though she secretly wished to flee. "Yes, I understand."

"Welcome to our restaurant," Kiaan said, flashing her a smile that revealed charming dimples. She was completely mesmerised; if she could, she would drop to her knees and propose to him right then and there.

"Thank you," she managed to reply, her voice barely above a whisper.

"Kay, this is Danny, our lead hand. He'll give you a tour and introduce you to the rest of the staff," he said, looking straight into her eyes.

"Sure. Thank you," Kavya replied, feeling a mix of intimidation and excitement as Kiaan hung up his apron and walked out of the kitchen.

"Okay, Kavya, let's get to work," Danny said, his voice friendly but firm. "Have you worked in a kitchen before?"

Kavya felt a wave of panic wash over her. She hadn't anticipated actually having to work, but here she was, stepping into the chaos of a professional kitchen. There were large pots and pans hanging overhead, and the atmosphere was alive with energy.

"No," she replied, her heart racing. She was regretting every second of this walk, but there was no turning back now.

"It's okay. You'll learn as you go," Danny reassured her. "It's a fast-paced environment; you won't even realise where the time goes. Meet Jessi, Ronald, and Maria. They'll help you out."

"Hello," Kavya whispered, forcing a smile despite the anxiety bubbling inside her. She could see the camaraderie among the staff, and it both comforted and intimidated her.

"Hello! Nice to meet you," Jessi, a short man with an inviting smile, greeted her warmly.

"You look nervous," Maria, an Italian woman in her late fifties with grey hair and a warm smile, said, patting Kavya's back. "Don't worry; it looks like a lot of work, but we all pitch in." Ronald, who appeared to be in his sixties, leaned against the counter. "Hello, my lady. Welcome to our kitchen! Think of this place as a big family. We've all been together for over ten years. You'll love it here—and hey, the food and drinks are all on the boss."

Kavya took a deep breath and felt her worries begin to fade. "Okay, let's start with the carrots," Danny said, grabbing a bunch and showing her where to begin.

"Here, the peeler," he instructed, gesturing towards the sink and a large container nearby.

Kavya took the bunch of carrots, her heart sinking as she realised it wasn't just one bunch but a daunting hundred of them. She felt ready to faint, but just then, Kiaan walked back into the kitchen.

"Are you ready, Kavya?" he asked, his gaze warm and encouraging.

Kavya quickly composed herself, forcing a smile. "Yes, I'm ready. Thank you for giving me the opportunity to work beside you." The blush creeping up her cheeks made her feel even more flustered.

"That's great, Kavya. We have an amazing team here. Let's start our day," Kiaan said, tying on his apron before heading into the walk-in freezer.

Kavya took a deep breath, grabbing the first carrot and beginning to peel. She couldn't believe she was really in the back of a restaurant kitchen, facing an enormous pile of carrots under the bright kitchen lights. "It's like a boot camp," she whispered to herself, trying to convince her racing mind that she could handle this.

As she peeled the carrots, she couldn't help but steal glances at Kiaan every chance she got. If she could, she would sit in front of him all day, just to look at him and admire his handsome features. There was something magnetic about him that drew her in, and she found herself captivated.

How would she ever tell him she was in love with him?

Just then, her thoughts were interrupted by loud laughter ringing through the kitchen. She turned to see five elegantly dressed women in black surrounding Kiaan. One woman was in his arms, while another leaned in to kiss him.

"What the hell?" she whispered, her heart sinking.

"Oh babe, those are the waitresses," Danny said, glancing at Kavya. She felt her cheeks flush, a mix of embarrassment and jealousy swirling inside her.

"Are you okay?" Danny asked, noticing her reaction.

"I'm fine," Kavya said, focusing intently on peeling the carrots, trying to suppress her rising emotions. "You don't look very well. You look a bit angry," Danny said, concern etched on his face.

"I said I'm fine, Danny," she snapped, handing him the peeler before walking away to find Maria. "Maria, can you please show me how to wash these cups in the machine? I haven't done this before," Kavya asked, determined to shift her focus away from her feelings.

"Oh yes, my baby. I can show you. It's easy," Maria replied, starting to load glasses into the industrial dishwasher.

"Thank you, Maria. You're so sweet. It does look like a lot of fun, especially with those waitresses around Kiaan," Kavya pointed out, trying to gauge Maria's thoughts. "Oh, those? Kiaan has a lot of women around him all the time. He's a player for sure," Maria said, winking at Kavya as she continued to load the dishes.

Kavya's heart sank. "Does he ever want to get married?" she asked, unable to hide her curiosity. "Oh darling, men like Kiaan never get married. He's looking for a woman who would bear his children, but he doesn't want to be tied down," Maria replied, shaking her head as she worked.

"What a strange man," Kavya sighed, feeling a mix of disappointment and determination. This was not what she had envisioned when she thought of winning Kiaan's heart.

As she took over the job of loading the glasses into the dishwasher, her mind raced. She pressed her chest and took a deep breath. All of this was for him? And all he wants is a woman to have his child? She shook her head, trying to focus on the task at hand. "There's a salad already cut in the fridge. Put it in the containers for takeout orders," Maria instructed, pointing to the clear plastic containers stacked nearby.

"Okay, sure," Kavya said, trying to shake off her conflicting thoughts. She walked to the fridge, determined to push through this challenge.

As she opened the fridge and pulled out a silver container filled with salad, she felt a sense of accomplishment. But then—

THUD!

A loud crash echoed through the kitchen as the giant container of salad tumbled from her hands and landed upside down on the floor. Suddenly, all activity ceased, and every pair of eyes in the kitchen turned to her. Kavya stood frozen, her heart pounding in her chest. Every nerve in her body tingled with fear. The silence was deafening, amplifying her feelings of dread as she struggled to calm her racing mind. Kiaan, who had been entertaining the waitresses, turned and walked towards her.

Kavya felt her stomach drop. How had she messed this up so quickly?

Kiaan bent down, picking up the scattered salad and placing it back into the bowl. Kavya knelt beside him, mortified but eager to help. "It's okay, Kavya. It's your first day. We'll make a fresh batch. Just throw this in the garbage," Kiaan said, his voice calm and reassuring as he sat beside her on the floor.

As they cleaned together, Kavya caught a whiff of his cologne, intoxicating and warm. She secretly glanced at him, admiring every handsome detail of his face—from his arched eyebrows and neatly trimmed beard to his curly eyelashes and full lips.

Ah, those dimples!

This was exactly where she wanted to be—close to him, even if it was while cleaning the floor.

Stacy Go Home!

The sound of excited barking filled the air as Kiaan tapped the number on his front door, anticipation coursing through him. As soon as the door swung open, a joyful pit bull with a glossy coat bounded towards him.

"Panda! My baby girl!" Kiaan exclaimed, dropping his bag on the hardwood floor and kneeling to embrace his beloved dog, Mia. The warmth of her fur and the wagging of her tail brought a smile to his face.

"Oh, what a beautiful dog!" a voice interrupted, and he looked up to see Stacy, one of the restaurant's waitresses, standing in the doorway. She wore a form-fitting black bodycon dress that accentuated her curves, her jacket draped over one arm and a handbag casually slung across her shoulder, hinting at her partially visible cleavage.

"Oh, she's my baby girl. A bit of a tough face, but a real softy," Kiaan said fondly, continuing to pet Panda as she nuzzled against him.

Suddenly, Panda jumped up, nearly knocking Stacy off her feet. She braced herself against the wall, laughter escaping her lips. "Oh, I'm sorry! She almost knocked you down. Please, come in," Kiaan said, holding Panda by her collar and giving her a gentle tap on the backside. "Panda, go to your bed."

With a reluctant wag of her tail, Panda trotted away, her ears back, retreating to her cosy spot in the living room. As Stacy stepped inside, her eyes widened at the sight of a large fish tank beautifully positioned against the wall of Kiaan's brownstone townhouse in Brooklyn. The colourful fish darted about, creating a serene ambience in the modern space.

"Oh wow! That's a very big fish tank," she remarked, genuinely impressed.

"Thank you," Kiaan replied, hanging his jacket on a nearby coat rack.

Stacy walked further into the living room, taking in the clean and elegant space—the white couches, the sparkling crystal chandelier overhead, and the sheer white drapes that framed the tall windows. "It's so clean and elegant. The white couches, the chandelier, and the carpet—it's like no one lives here!"

"Well, no one does besides me and the dog," he said with a chuckle. "Can I make you a drink? Looks like the drive has sobered you up."

"Oh yes, I could definitely use another drink," Stacy laughed, her eyes sparkling with mischief.

"Ha! You're a funny girl, Stacy. Come over here," Kiaan said, moving towards the kitchen.

He began to prepare a martini. Stacy hopped onto the marble countertop, her legs swinging playfully. Kiaan mixed the drink with practised ease and soon handed it to her.

"Cheers!" she said with a grin, taking a sip, her eyes dancing with delight.

Before she knew it, Kiaan leaned in and captured her lips with his in a soft kiss. As he slipped his hand under her dress, Stacy opened her legs slightly, still savouring her martini.

"You're a naughty boy, Kiaan," she teased, wrapping her arms around his neck and leaning in, pressing her lips against his once more.

With a flick of the remote, Kiaan dimmed the lights in the living room, creating an intimate atmosphere. He lifted Stacy effortlessly into his arms, grabbing a bottle of vodka with one hand before striding into the living room. He placed her gently onto the couch, where she set her glass on the table.

No words were exchanged as the tension hung thick in the air. Stacy, now sitting in her thong and pink bra, felt the electricity between them. Kiaan took her feet into his hands, gently rubbing them before kissing her toes, slowly moving up to her legs.

"So, that new girl you have in the kitchen—what's her name?" Stacy asked, breaking the silence as she took another sip of her martini.

"The dishwasher and kitchen helper?" Kiaan replied, shifting his position slightly.

"Yes! She doesn't look like she's ever worked in a kitchen before, and she's very pretty," Stacy observed, a hint of curiosity in her tone.

"What makes you say that?" Kiaan asked, arching an eyebrow.

"Well, a lot of things. For starters, she dropped a salad," Stacy said, smirking. "That was an accident," Kiaan countered, slightly defensive.

"Right, but she's wearing a Tiffany pendant, her nails are perfectly polished, and there's not a muscle in her arms," Stacy pointed out, her voice dripping with scepticism.

"Oh, so? What's up with that? Seems normal to me," Kiaan shrugged, feeling a bit annoyed.

"She was watching us leave from the window. I thought that was kind of creepy. Like she is your girlfriend or something," Stacy continued, her eyes narrowing slightly.

"Didn't they all? They all look at us or me leaving with women? Even you have watched me leave with girls before, no?" Kiaan replied, his hand going between her legs.

"Kiaan, you're not listening to me," Stacy said, trying to regain his attention. But as Kiaan began kissing her neck, her protest faded away. Kiaan slid his hand beneath her dress, pulling her thong down. Stacy lifted her body, allowing him access. In the midst of their passionate embrace, her drink slipped from her hand, splattering across the pristine white carpet.

Kiaan froze, his eyes widening at the mess. He quickly stood up, looking down at the stain on his once-pristine carpet. A pang of regret coursed through him as he glanced at Stacy's delicate lace thong before returning it to her, feeling a mix of disappointment and irritation.

"Stacy, my love, I must ask you to depart," Kiaan murmured, his voice heavy with regret.

"I'm sorry, Kiaan. I didn't do it intentionally," she said, rising from the couch, her demeanour shifting.

"It's not you, babe. It's just that today has been another tough one," he said softly, kissing her neck as he reached for his phone to call an Uber.

Stacy quickly dressed, slipping into her clothes while Kiaan helped her put her shoes on. He grabbed a water bottle and handed it to her.

"Your cab is here. This water bottle is for your ride home," he said, leaning in to kiss her once more.

"Aww, you're so caring. Is that why all the women drool over you?" she teased, her voice playful but slightly slurred from the drinks.

Kiaan smiled, helping her into the waiting Uber. "See you at work tomorrow," he said, kissing her gently on the lips as the cab pulled away.

He watched the car disappear down the street; a heavy sigh escaped him. He looked down at the stain on the carpet, a reminder of the night's reckless abandon and the complicated emotions swirling within him. It was just another night in the life of a chef—filled with fleeting moments and lingering regrets.

How Much Do You Make?

Phone rings. "Wake up, Mia." It was 1 pm in New York, and the weight of the previous day's work pressed heavily on Kavya.

She sighed, feeling the ache in her muscles from her first shift in the kitchen. "You think I can just get out of bed after all the work I did yesterday?" she replied to Mia, whose voice was crackling through the phone.

"It's not really a good choice to start dishwashing because you fell in love with some dude you don't even know," Mia shot back, her tone teasing yet firm as she strolled down the bustling streets of New York, shopping bags swinging from her arms.

"Mia, I'm sore. I can't afford this speech right now. Why are you calling?" Kavya groaned, pulling the sheets tighter around her as if they could shield her from the world.

She had a few hours left before she needed to head back to her new job, and all she wanted was to sleep. "I want you to come have lunch with me. I did some shopping," Mia insisted, her excitement palpable even through the phone. She was dressed in a chic suit, perfectly tailored to accentuate her figure, and she was seated at a stylish restaurant downtown, surrounded by the vibrant energy of the city. "I can't. I just want to sleep before I go back to work," Kavya replied, glancing at the blackout blinds that kept her room in a perpetual twilight. "Fine. Be that way," Mia huffed, hanging up the phone with a click that echoed in Kavya's ears.

Meanwhile, Mia sat at her booth, her shopping bags piled beside her, the elegant surroundings of the restaurant a stark contrast to Kavya's dim room. Just then, a handsome server approached her table. He wore a crisp white shirt and black pants that highlighted his muscular physique, and his piercing blue eyes caught her attention immediately. "Can I get you a drink to start with?" he asked, flashing a charming smile. "Could I please have a Part-time Lover's Martini? Thank you," Mia replied, her voice laced with a hint of flirtation as she admired him.

"Of course. I'll give you a few more minutes to decide on your dinner. I'll be right back with your drink," he said before stepping away. "Excuse me," Mia called after him, wanting to change her seating arrangement. "Yes, ma'am?" He turned back, his expression attentive. "Oh, I was wondering if I could move to the bar. My sister isn't coming for lunch, and I don't wish to hog the whole table alone," she explained. The server smiled, taking her water glass and menu.

"Sure. I'll escort you to the bar, madam," he guided her through the restaurant, placing her glass and menu on the bar counter. "Thank you," Mia smiled, feeling the excitement of the bustling atmosphere around her.

"Your drink will be here shortly," he assured her before walking away. Mia took out her laptop and set it on the counter, turning it on as she settled into her new space.

The bar was lively, filled with patrons enjoying their meals and drinks, and she couldn't help but feel a sense of comfort in the chaos. "Oh, hello. How are you doing this afternoon?" she heard a voice from behind her.

It was the bartender, an African-American man dressed in a blue shirt with the top buttons undone, revealing a silver chain around his neck. His neatly cut hair and the bracelet on his wrist added to his charm. "Oh, the noon is going well. Thank you. Just took off from work early," she replied, scrolling through her emails, deliberately avoiding eye contact.

"Well, that's awesome. Can I get you a drink?" he asked, his brown eyes sparkling with interest. "I already requested one, but can I get a gin and tonic?" she said, not wanting to refuse his offer.

She noticed his curly eyelashes framing his warm gaze. "I'll be right back with your drink," he said, flashing her a smile before moving on to the next customer. The bar began to fill up. Mia focused on her laptop, slipping on her glasses to read through her emails. Moments later, the bartender returned with her gin and tonic.

"Here's your drink," he said, placing it in front of her. "Thank you, James. Actually, I have decided that I'll be getting some food," she said, glancing at his name tag. "Yes, what can I get you to eat?" he asked, pulling out a pen and notepad.

"Let's keep it simple: I'll have the steak and mashed potatoes on the side," she said, handing the menu back to him. "Sure. I'll be right back," Danny replied before disappearing into the kitchen. Mia removed her earbuds, tucking them away in her purse as she prepared to enjoy her meal. She took a sip of her gin and tonic, savouring the refreshing taste. Half an hour later, her dinner arrived, the steak glistening and perfectly cooked.

She closed her laptop and placed her glasses aside, ready to dig in. Just then, a man moved next to her at the bar.

"May I?" he asked, his tone polite. The man was in his late thirties, with an average build, a light beard, fair skin, and striking blue eyes.

Mia vaguely heard him through her music and responded, "You may."

She took her earbuds out and tucked them back into her green Prada purse, her shopping bags resting at her feet.

"So, how are you today?" the man asked, taking a sip from his beer. "It's busy," she replied, cutting a piece of her juicy steak and popping it into her mouth. "Well, you're alone?" he observed, leaning in slightly.

"I can't be alone?" she shot back, her tone defensive as she continued to eat.

"You can, but can I join you?" he asked, a hint of charm in his voice. Mia took a sip of her drink, considering her options. She remained silent for a moment, focusing on her food.

"I'm Luke," he introduced himself, extending a hand. Still chewing her steak, Mia finished her bite and wiped her mouth with a napkin before placing it on the table.

"So, Luke. What's your annual income?" she asked bluntly, her curiosity piqued. "Excuse me?" he looked taken aback, placing his drink down.

"Yes. How much do you earn annually?" she pressed, her eyes narrowing slightly.

"Why does that matter?" Luke asked, raising an eyebrow. "It does. I want to know if my time is worth spending on this conversation," she replied, her tone nonchalant as she took the last sip of her drink.

"That's a very rude question," Luke said, a frown forming on his face. "James, I'll take the bill," she called out, ignoring Luke's discomfort.

"How would you like to pay?" James asked, handing her the bill along with the payment machine.

She pulled out her black American Express card and tapped it against the machine, feeling the weight of the moment. "Do you need a receipt?" James asked.

"No, thank you very much, James," she replied, slipping the card back into her Hermès bag while gathering her shopping bags.

"You know what's rude, Luke? To interfere with someone having a perfect lunch alone. Have a great day," Mia said, her voice firm as she turned and walked out of the restaurant, leaving Luke staring after her, his expression a mix of confusion and irritation.

She stepped back into the bustling streets of New York, the city. There was a wide smile on the plastic surgeon's face.

Challenging Me?

“Liam, can you please help me with the bags upstairs?” Mia stepped out of her Uber, her heels clicking on the pavement as she navigated the bustling street.

“Of course. Let me take those bags for you,” Liam, the doorman, smiled as he took the heavy bags from her slender arms and gestured towards the elevator. “Thank you, Liam,” Mia replied, her tone warm but distracted. She entered the luxurious penthouse, the scent of fresh espresso wafting through the air.

“You’re welcome, Mia. Have a great day,” Liam called as he stepped back into the elevator, the doors sliding shut with a soft ‘ding’.

As Mia walked into the living room, she found her sister Kavya lounging on a plush chair, her fingers dancing over the keyboard of her laptop.

"Shopping? Have you got me anything?" Kavya looked up, her eyes sparkling with anticipation.

"No. But you could have come," Mia replied, walking to the kitchen to prepare herself a rich espresso.

"You called me for lunch, not shopping, Mia," Kavya retorted, rolling her eyes playfully.

"It was a very tasty steak with a side of mashed potatoes," Mia said, a smirk playing on her lips as she pulled a pair of shoes out of a shopping bag. She slipped them on, admiring her reflection in the mirror.

"I'm sore. I have to go back to work in a couple of hours," Kavya groaned, rubbing her shoulder as if to ease the tension.

"Dude, you know you're crazy for going through all this for a man?" Mia took off her designer sunglasses, placing them delicately on the side table.

"If I fly on vacation, I want to fly with him. If I take a road trip, I want to wake up beside him and go to bed with him at night. I want to lay my head on his chest and fall asleep. I'm really in love with him, Mia," Kavya's voice is earnest, her eyes filled with a mix of longing and hope.

"Teenager stuff, Kav. You barely know him! You saw him once, and now you're saying you love him?" Mia rolled her eyes, a hint of disbelief in her tone.

"I know him! He's handsome, successful, a chef who owns a restaurant, and on top of that, all women like him. He's like a perfect package!" Kavya stood, moving towards the coffee machine, limping on her leg.

"Oh, look at you walking as if someone just beat you up or something," Mia teased, a playful smirk on her face.

"Mias, please, can we be supportive about this?" Kavya pleaded, her voice serious now.

"You just said all women like him? So, is he a player?" Mia raised an eyebrow; her curiosity mingled with concern.

"Oh, that's a little more complicated than that," Kavya responded, her expression growing sombre.

"In what sense? Seems pretty straightforward to me. You could just show up as who you really are—rich and wealthy—and he'd marry you in a heartbeat." Mia's tone was sharp, her frustration evident.

"Yes, that's the complication! Marry anyone in a heartbeat? He's a player, and he just wants to pay a woman to have her kid and pay her to raise the child.

He has no intentions of ever getting married!" Kavya looked at Mia, her eyes searching for understanding.

Silence hung heavily in the air.

"Mias?" Kavya prompted, breaking the tension.

"Babe, I'm just very confused here. You're working in the back of the kitchen for a man who's a player and doesn't want to settle down? I'm trying to understand this," Mia's face twisted in a mask of anger, her eyes flashing with fury.

"Mias, love doesn't have to make any sense. It just happens! When you're in love, you can move mountains," Kavya's voice had passion, but she avoided making eye contact.

"My love, I'm not saying you shouldn't love, but this is madness. It feels like infatuation towards a man who clearly has no interest in commitment," Mia insisted, her voice raising slightly.

"Why are we jumping to marrying him? I just want to date the man first, cuddle him," Kavya looked at Mia, her eyes narrowing slightly.

"Then you could just walk into the restaurant and ask him out for a date. You said he likes pretty girls. You're pretty, rich, and indeed famous," Mia countered, her tone now laced with sarcasm.

"You know you won't understand me. I don't want him to love me for who my parents are. I want him to love me for who I am!" Kavya's voice trembled with emotion, her frustration evident.

"And you're a dishwasher in his kitchen!" Mia laughed sarcastically, the sound echoing off the walls.

Kavya remained silent, her expression hardened as she processed Mia's words.

"I'm going upstairs," Kavya finally said, her voice tight with suppressed emotion.

As she moved towards the staircase, she glanced back at Mia, who sat on the couch with an air of disappointment about her.

"Why don't you get in the game and see who wins the man?" Kavya challenged, her face devoid of emotion, a blank slate that contrasted with the storm of feelings swirling inside her.

"Excuse me? You're challenging me?" Mia's shock was palpable, her mind racing to reconcile this boldness from her younger sister, who seemed not so long ago to be a little girl playing with dolls.

The memories flooded back—together they played with Barbies shared secrets in their playroom and wore hand-knitted sweaters made by their grandmother in a mansion filled with love. Yet now, they stood on opposite sides of a battlefield, neither of them had anticipated such a day.

"I am indeed challenging you, Mias. Make this man fall in love with you, and let's see who wins. It's so easy, right? Just walk in and ask him out? Besides, you're cold and icy anyway," Kavya took one more step up the stairs, her voice taunting yet laced with an undertone of desperation.

"I am not cold, Kav! Stop this nonsense!" Mia's voice dropped an octave, the weight of the conversation pressing down on her.

"Fun and games? I have a super busy schedule, but hey, challenge accepted," Mia replied, her gaze locking onto Kavya's, a fire igniting within her.

"Good luck, sister. True love always wins. I have to get ready for work. See you," Kavya said and turned her back as she walked up the stairs, leaving Mia to stew in the tension.

"It isn't love, just infatuation. Good night," Mia shook her head in disappointment, her shoulders dropping as she exhaled deeply. Plastic surgeons don't have time for games, but somehow, she's now embroiled in one with the cousin she loves so dearly. The challenge loomed over her, a silent battle of hearts, and she can't help but wonder if she's truly ready to enter the fray.

Love Bombing

"Maria, there's a note on my desk. Do you know who put it there?" Kiaan stepped out of his office, a small pink slip crumpled in his hand.

"What kind of note?" Maria asked, her curiosity piqued.

"This," he replied, handing the note to her.

"Oh boy. This is a love note! 'I love you, Kiaan. I love you to the moon and back a million times!'" Maria read aloud, her voice teasing as she flipped the note over. "Just the thought of you in my mind makes me run in circles." She handed the note back to Kiaan, a big smile on her face.

"Who put this here? There's no name on it," Kiaan frowned, scanning the kitchen where his helpers were working diligently. Kavya, busy loading dishes into the dishwasher, catches the exchange out of the corner of her eye, her heart racing.

"All the other times, I usually know who's going nuts over me," he continued, glancing at the note with a bemused smile before tossing it in the garbage.

Kavya watched silently, her stomach twisting as she felt Kiaan's presence draw nearer. He strode towards her with purpose, and for a split second, Kavya's heart plummeted—she thought he was coming to fire her.

Her mouth went dry, and she crossed her fingers in the soapy water, bubbles forming around her hands. "Kav, Stacy called in sick. Think you could serve today?" Kiaan asked, his voice warm and inviting as he closed the distance between them.

Hesitantly, Kavya responded, "I've never seen Mia before," setting the cup down on the dish rack, trying to steady her breath.

'There's always a first time for everything, right?' Kiaan replied, his gaze locked onto hers, leaning in just enough such that she could feel the heat radiating from him. He towered over her, making her feel small yet safe in his presence.

Kavya nodded, her heart fluttering.

She was in love with her charming boss, and she'd do anything for him.

"Okay then, please grab an apron. Thank you so much for covering for Stacy," Kiaan.

Kavya nodded again, her excitement mingled with nerves. She grabbed an apron, her hands trembling slightly as she tied it around her waist. The kitchen, usually chaotic and uninviting, felt transformed; it was now the most beautiful place on earth because Kiaan was there.

After three exhausting hours of serving, Kavya finally called it a day. She removed her apron and shrugged on her jacket, fatigue washing over her as she headed towards the exit. The first thing her eyes landed on was Kiaan's sleek Maserati parked out front.

With a quick touch-up of her lipstick, she leaned in and pressed a kiss onto the icy cold, frosted window of his car, completely unaware of the frigid temperature.

As she stood there, her heart raced; she felt a wave of panic wash over her—what if someone saw her? She quickly blew warm air onto the window, trying to create a more noticeable mark. After a few moments, she stepped back, admiring the faint lipstick imprint left behind. Encouraged, she dared to make more, each time blowing warm air onto the glass to help her mark stand out.

Silently, she hoped Kiaan would notice these little kisses on his car. Just then, Maria opened the door and tossed out the garbage. "Honey, are you okay?" she asked, noticing Kavya standing alone in the back parking lot. "I'm fine, just waiting for my cab," Kavya replied, relieved that Maria didn't see her leaving kisses on Kiaan's car.

"Okay! If you want, I can drop you off. Where do you live?" Maria offered, her tone friendly. Kavya almost blurted out, "Penthouse on the Upper East Side," but she caught herself.

"It's okay, Maria. Thank you, but I'll make it home myself. I appreciate your offer," she rubbed her hands together, trying to warm up in the chilly air. "Alright. Have a good night!" Maria called as she headed back inside the restaurant. Kavya let out a deep sigh, grateful that Maria didn't witness her little secret. She glanced back at Kiaan's Maserati one last time. The window looked utterly lonesome, and a flutter of butterflies took flight in her stomach. It seemed silly, but she was relishing this thrill, feeling like a lovestruck teenager trying to win over the heart of her crush. But was she trying too hard? Just the thought sent a wave of uncertainty through her, but for now, she couldn't help but smile at the risk of it all.

The Date!

“Excuse me!” Mia called out, her voice smooth and confident, as she sat elegantly at a dimly lit table in the restaurant.

She’s wearing a white bodycon dress that hugged her curves, accentuated by a push-up bra that enhanced her silhouette. Her long hair cascaded over her shoulders, framing her face perfectly. Next to her, a luxurious green Hermès purse rested casually, a testament to her affluent lifestyle.

She set her spoon down, the soft clink echoing in the quiet ambience, and waved to a server strolling by. “Yes, ma’am. How may I assist you?” the server replied, approaching her table with a polite smile. “I was wondering if I could speak to the chef,” she requested, a playful challenge sparkling in her eyes.

Mia had accepted Kavya's dare: she intended to make Kiaan fall for her. "Oh, certainly, ma'am. I'll get the chef right away," the server said, turning on his heel and heading towards the kitchen.

Moments later, Kiaan emerged, his tall frame commanding attention as he strode confidently towards her table.

"Good evening! How can I help you?" he asked, his tone warm and welcoming. "This dinner is absolutely amazing! I just had to meet the genius behind it. The ambience is simply glorious," Mia beamed, her smile brightening her face.

"Thank you so much! I'm thrilled to hear that you enjoyed our dining experience. It's always a pleasure to know our guests appreciate the effort and passion we put into creating these dishes," Kiaan responded, standing tall and placing his hands together in a gesture of modesty, his cheeks slightly flushed by her compliment.

"Well, you're definitely a New York gem," Mia said, raising an eyebrow flirtatiously. "Thank you!" Kiaan replied as his earlier blush deepened. "I was wondering, would you like to join me for drinks after closing? It's almost time," she suggested, leaning forward slightly, her eyes locking onto his, confident that her alluring appearance would sway him. "Oh, yes, sure! I'm flattered," Kiaan stammered, clearly taken by her boldness.

"Great! I'll wait for you to finish up," Mia said, crossing her legs and handing him her phone. Kiaan took the phone and quickly entered his number before returning it to her.

She smiled, a spark of excitement dancing in her eyes. "I'll be right back. Let me just speak to my staff," Kiaan said, glancing at her one last time before heading back to the kitchen. Fifteen minutes later, Kiaan returned, putting on his coat as he walked back to Mia's table.

A few guests lingered around, but the atmosphere was intimate, almost electric. He extended his hand, gracefully offering assistance as she rose to her feet. Together, they made their way to his Maserati parked outside. "Oh!" Kiaan exclaimed, noticing the frosted windows adorned with lipstick marks. "What happened?" Mia asked innocently as walked over to the driver's side to inspect the window, a smile creeping onto her face. "What's wrong?" Kiaan asked, confusion etched across his features as he examined the affectionate marks on his car.

"Oh, it's cute! Do you have some secret admirers?" she teased, raising an eyebrow playfully. "I'm not sure who did this. We can check the surveillance cameras tomorrow," Kiaan replied, his brow furrowing slightly as he walked.

Mia went to the passenger side and opened the door for her. "Oh, come on. It's just lipstick. Take some paper and Windex and wipe it off. Unless you're trying to justify something?" Mia quipped, a sly smile on her lips.

"Yeah, whatever. I just think this is very childish," Kiaan muttered, getting into the car and pretending to ignore the marks, even as his ears turned red. Mia's lips curved into a subtle smile, a flicker of amusement dancing in her eyes.

He had a hunch about the identity of the mysterious individual who left those kisses on his car. "So, where shall I drive you at this late hour, Miss?" Kiaan inquired, his gaze resting on her with curiosity. They were together throughout the evening; they have yet to exchange names.

"Oh, right! Call me Mias," she replied, extending her hand for a formal handshake. Kiaan took her hand and kissed it gently. "Kiaan," he whispered, his voice low. Mia pulled her hand back, a thrill coursing through her. "So, what's on your mind?" "Well, we could go to my place," Kiaan suggests, his tone casual, yet there's an underlying tension in the air.

Mia opened her Hermès bag and pulled out a shimmering lip gloss, applying it carefully as she smudged her lips together. "Wouldn't that be a bit too fast? I think we just met," she raised an eyebrow, a teasing lilt in her voice.

Kiaan chuckled, starting the Maserati's engine. "It's loud," Mia commented, glancing out the window. "Your neighbours don't mind you driving this late at night and disrupting their sleep?"

"Good question. I only drive it once in a while," he responded, stealing a glance at her. "There's not really a plan, to be honest. I thought you were hot," she said, her gaze sliding from his chest to his eyes, a flirtatious smirk playing on her lips.

"So we can go to my place and hang out. You can stay over if you like," Kiaan proposed, his expression hopeful. "That would be convenient, but I don't like the idea of drinking if I'm supposed to go there for a fun evening. You see, we just shook hands," she replied, her words laced with playful flirtation.

"Fine, we can play video games," Kiaan suggested, his tone light. "Okay, sure! That sounds like a good plan," Mia agreed, her heart racing with anticipation. Kiaan pulled out into the bustling streets of New York, the sounds of the city intertwining with the roar of his Maserati, creating a symphony of the night—a New York lullaby.

A Regular Man

Kiaan led Mia into his cosy Brooklyn abode, the warm glow of soft lighting creating an inviting atmosphere. "You have a very elegant space," Mia remarked, taking in the tasteful décor and the comfortable vibe of the home. After settling into the living room, she placed her Hermès purse on the coffee table, its luxurious green leather gleaming under the lights.

"Would you like something to drink?" Kiaan asked, glancing at her with curiosity.

"I think I could use some coffee to keep me awake," she smiled, sinking into the plush white couch. "Of course! I can make you a very special espresso," Kiaan replied, moving towards the kitchen with a spring in his step.

As he prepared the coffee, Mia took the opportunity to engage him in conversation. "The woman who will marry you will be a happy girl," she said, her tone light and teasing.

Kiaan chuckled softly, shaking his head. "Well, I'm not getting married ever, so there isn't a lucky girl, I guess," he answered, his gaze focused on the coffee machine.

Mia stood up from the couch and walked over to him, intrigued. "And why is that?" she asked, tilting her head slightly.

"Who wants to give up on all these pretty girls and settle down with just one?" Kiaan replied, avoiding eye contact as he poured steaming coffee into a cup. "Every time I meet a new girl, it feels like a fresh start. Marriage just goes stale and saggy over time." He handed her the cup, a slight smile on his face.

"So, I'm all alone in a player's house?" Mia teased, raising an eyebrow as she took the mug from him. "Yes. A pretty woman has landed in my house, that's for sure. But don't worry, I'm a gentleman. A woman's permission is a must," he said with a wink.

Mia took a sip of her coffee, savouring the rich flavour. "But you'll never have a soulmate? Wouldn't you want someone to share your best moments with, like having a baby and raising it together?" she asked, her curiosity piqued.

"Let's get to the fun part and head to my game room," Kiaan suggested, clearly trying to redirect the conversation. "Sorry if I asked a personal question," Mia replied, following him to the game room.

"It's not that personal. I just don't see how soulmates work anymore. All I see are people living day by day with partners they're with for kids or financial reasons. In 2024, I see more cheaters and users than true love," Kiaan expressed, his eyes meeting hers with a hint of vulnerability.

"Oh boy! Looks like someone's been hurt," Mia said playfully as they entered the game room, which featured a big projector screen and comfortable recliner couches.

Kiaan remained quiet; his expression thoughtful. "Do you have any game preferences?" he asked, turning on the console.

"Minecraft!" Mia exclaimed, finishing her coffee and placing the empty mug on the table. Little did she know, Kiaan was a Minecraft mastermind, possessing an incredible talent for crafting elaborate structures in the game.

'Sure!' he replied, a confident smile spreading across his face. As they played, Kiaan revealed, 'My parents are divorced. I grew up watching them argue and fight all the time.'

Mia paused for a moment, processing his words. "Sorry to hear that," she said softly, focusing back on the game. As they delved into Minecraft, Mia was amazed by Kiaan's skills. He built towering castles, intricate redstone contraptions, and even a pixelated replica of his restaurant.

Meanwhile, Mia struggled to place a single block without it tumbling down in a humorous fashion. Despite her lack of gaming prowess, she laughed at the absurdity of it all—here she was, in the home of a talented chef turned virtual architect, trying her best to keep up with his creativity.

After about half an hour, she sighed, "Okay, I think I need to head home and get some sleep. I have an early meeting in the morning." "You never told me what you do. I see that Hermès purse you're carrying," Kiaan said with a playful wink.

"I'm an insurance agent," she replied, her focus still on the screen. "Oh, must be a good one to have a £45k Birkin bag," Kiaan commented, his gaze drifting over her figure adorned in the bodycon dress.

His eyes roamed from her elegant attire to the way her hair framed her face, then down to the subtle curves that caught his attention.

“That’s what exes are for, isn’t it?” Mia quipped, still focused on the game, and Kiaan’s interest seemed piqued.

“Are you drooling?” she asked playfully, glancing at him for a moment. “Maybe,” Kiaan admitted, putting down his controller and leaning closer to her.

Mia set her controller down, captivated by his mesmerising eyes. For a fleeting moment, she felt an overwhelming urge to lean into him and surrender to the growing chemistry, but she reminded herself that they were still in the game.

Kiaan moved closer, his face just inches from hers. Mia placed her hand gently on his chest, halting him. The strength of his well-built physique was evident beneath her touch.

‘What’s wrong?’ Kiaan asked, sitting back slightly. ‘I just think it’s too late. I need to go. You know I have work tomorrow,’ Mia said, her voice tinged with reluctance.

“Sure, my lady. Should I drop you off?” he asked, concern in his tone.

“No, it’s okay. I’ll just Uber home,” she replied, pulling out her phone to request a ride. “It’s only three minutes away,” he said, watching her as she got up and put on her Burberry jacket and Prada boots.

“You’re not really an insurance agent, are you? You lied, right?” Kiaan stood by the door; curiosity etched on his face as Mia's hair fell over her eyes while she slipped into her shoes.

She stood tall, placing her Birkin bag on her arm and smiled coyly. "I am a doctor."

"I don't know which of your stories is true. You're too hot to be a doctor. Don't they usually look like nerds?" Kiaan teased, his dimples deepening as he grinned.

"Let you choose! Do you want to hang out with an insurance agent or a doctor? Whatever pleases you. I had a good time," she said, giving Kiaan a warm hug before walking out through the grand oak doors to catch her Uber.

Kiaan stood at his door, watching Mia disappear into the vibrant streets of Brooklyn, a mix of emotions swirling in his chest. He couldn't shake the feeling that the night had been special, and as he closed the door, he couldn't help but wonder if he'd see her again.

It's Just a game!

"You left kiss marks on his car?" Mia asked incredulously, dropping her keys onto the table with a clatter.

Kavya, seated on the couch with a plate of food from the restaurant, nodded her head in agreement, a mischievous smile playing on her lips. "Kav, are you crazy? That's vandalism!"

Mia expresses her concern, her voice rising slightly. Kavya shrugged nonchalantly, taking another bite of her food, the sound of her munching echoing in the quiet room. "This isn't India, where your dad can use his connections to get you out of trouble," Mia warned, crossing her arms. Kavya rolled her eyes, clearly unfazed.

"What are you even eating?" Mia probed again, her annoyance growing. "Food," Kavya replied dismissively, chewing as she focused on her plate. "Kav, seriously. What's wrong with you?" Mia persisted, frustration bubbling beneath the surface. "I'm eating food that Kiaan cooked," Kavya said, her tone defensive. The sound of her chewing was irritating, but right now, she felt more irritated by Mia's questions.

"Why can't you just be nice?" Mia snapped, her patience wearing thin. "How did you even know I left a kiss?" Kavya asked, her eyebrows arching in surprise as she put her spoon down on the plate.

"I had dinner at the restaurant and then went to his place," Mia explained, her tone casual.

"And?" Kavya set her plate on the coffee table, her interest piqued. "And what? We just played video games," Mia replied calmly.

"I cleaned dishes and mopped the floor. It's been a few weeks, and I already have blisters on my hands and feet. I can't even feel them after five hours. And you just waltz in, eat, and end up at his house?" Kavya's frustration spills over.

"Why are you mad? You chose this path for yourself. You could have done the same, Kav. Why are you being so dramatic?" Mia responded, confused by her cousin's outburst.

"You're my big sister. Why would you go to his place after just meeting him, especially when you know I love him?' Kavya raised her voice, hurt and anger mingling.

"Stop it, Kavya! We're not going to argue over a man. This is jealousy talking, and you know it. You agree he's a player," Mia stood firm, placing her hands on her hips.

"I never said he was a player!" Kavya retorted, her eyes wide with indignation. "People have red flags, Kavya. In his case, he's basically a walking red flag. Just go to bed. You're really pissing me off," Mia replied, taking a sip of her water, her frustration evident.

"You know what? Don't tell me anything next time. You do you. I will win him over," Kavya got up and left.

Mia shook her head in annoyance, "Okay. I will make him fall in love with me and crush his heart under my feet." Mia had an evil smile on her face. She was so sure she would never fall in love with a player.

The night was dark and the rain was pattering against the windows, the tension between them was even more palpable. Kavya was consumed with love for Kiaan, while Mia's mind raced with thoughts of how to make his life a living hell for treating women like toys.

Mia picks up her phone, her fingers hovering over the screen. She types out a quick message to Kiaan: "I'm home now. Thank you for the wonderful evening." Within 30 seconds, she got an instant reply, as if he had been waiting for her text.

"Glad to hear, my lady. Maybe we can meet again?" Mia's lips curled into a smile as she typed back, "I'm attending an art exhibition for one of my clients in downtown New York. You're most welcome to join me." A wicked grin spreads across her face as she hits send.

The thought of disrupting Kiaan's life filled her with a sense of glee. DESTROY HIS PEACE! was the only mantra echoing in her mind. How could a man who is a player, a womaniser, and an ass be knowledgeable about something as refined as art?

She chuckled to herself, imagining all the ways she could toy with his emotions.

Meanwhile, Kavya lay in her bed, scrolling through Kiaan's Instagram profile, her heart racing. She gazed at his handsome face, disbelief flooding her as she thought about how deeply she had fallen for him.

Leaning in, she kissed the screen, then pressed the phone against her chest, letting out a deep sigh. "Oh Kiaan, if I could buy you, I would pay any price. But that's not possible," she murmured, kissing his photo again. "I know I will make you mine. You belong to me and no one else. Once you see how love can change people, you will change too. Then we can get married and live happily ever after," she whispered to the phone, her heart full of hope. Exhausted from the day's work, she soon drifted off to sleep, dreaming of him.

Both cousins were lost in their own worlds: one consumed by love and yearning, the other fuelled by a desire for revenge. The penthouse felt hollow with only the distant sounds of fire trucks and ambulances punctuating the silence. Little did they know, a war had begun—a battle between two women, each dreaming of the same man while lying in their beds, unaware of the impending clash over Kiaan's heart.

Grand I Love You

"You can lift this! It's not that heavy," Maria insisted, showing Kavya a large bucket of feta cheese that must weigh around 25 kilograms. Kavya stared at the bucket, her eyes wide with disbelief.

It certainly looked heavy. She shook her head, indicating she couldn't manage it. "Look, I'll show you," Maria said confidently, bending down to lift the white bucket with ease. She walked over to the freezer with her short legs and set it down on the ground.

"See?" Maria tapped Kavya on the shoulder, a playful grin on her face. "You can do it too!" Kavya smiled but felt a strange sense of determination. Taking a deep breath, she stepped up to grab the remaining three buckets and, for a moment, felt lightheaded.

Just as she was about to lose her balance, her eyes darted towards Kiaan, who was chatting with a tall blonde woman. The sight of them together ignited a familiar pang of jealousy in her chest. If envy could produce smoke, Kavya would need a chimney above her head.

"Thank you, Maria," she mumbled, her gaze still fixed on Kiaan. "There is only one queen," she reminded herself, trying not to react to the woman who seemed to be hovering over Kiaan. Suddenly, the noise of the kitchen faded into the background as Kavya's focus narrowed solely on Kiaan.

Every time he walked by, she felt a rush of chill course through her body. Some days, she wished she could run to him and give him a tight hug; he appeared so strong and comforting in her imagination. But how could she ever tell him about her feelings? Her mind raced with ideas to get closer to him. Then it hit her—she could send him a "love letter."

What a perfect, low-pressure way to express her feelings without having to confront him directly. With a spark of inspiration, Kavya quickly searched for something on her phone before returning to her dishwashing duties. As the evening approached, the restaurant began to buzz with activity. Kiaan and the rest of the staff are busy preparing for the dinner rush.

About an hour later, Danny walked into the kitchen, clipboard in hand. "Kiaan, you have a delivery!" "You're the inventory guy? Deal with it," Kiaan replied, not looking up from his task. "It's a personal delivery. You have to come to see this," Danny insisted, his curiosity piqued. "Delivery for me? At my restaurant?" Kiaan raised an eyebrow and set down his apron as he headed towards the entrance.

"Hello! How can I help you?" Kiaan asked the man standing outside, who was holding a bunch of red heart-shaped balloons. "Sir, these are for you. Someone ordered 500 red balloons for you," the delivery man replied, glancing at the three men who were struggling to hold all the balloons. "Are you sure? Is this the correct address?"

Kiaan asked, bewildered as he assessed the scene. "Kiaan, right?" one of the delivery men confirmed, showing the order on a handheld device. "Yes. Do you have the sender's information?"

Kiaan inquires, still confused. "No, sir. I just got your address," the delivery man explained. "Alright, let's bring them in for now," Kiaan said, scratching his head as he decided to deal with the unexpected delivery. The three men bring all the balloons inside the restaurant, and the entire kitchen staff gathers in the front to see the spectacle. The sight of 500 heart-shaped balloons with

"I Love You" written on them takes everyone by surprise. Kavya watched the scene unfold, her heart racing.

No one suspected that she sent the balloons; a kitchen helper couldn't possibly be this extravagant, could she? "Oh, this is quite the grand declaration of love!" Jessie exclaimed, his eyes wide in astonishment. "Who would do something like this? It's so cheesy," Jessie added with a hint of disbelief.

"Does anyone know who sent this to me?" Kiaan asked, concern etched on his forehead as he scanned the crowd, his hands clenching tightly. "What's there to be stressed about?" Maria questioned, stepping closer to Kiaan. "What am I supposed to do with all these balloons?" Kiaan expressed his worry, looking overwhelmed.

"Cut the ribbons and let them hang from the ceiling? Our customers will enjoy the love bomb you've received, Kiaan!" Ronald joked, trying to lighten the mood. "Sure, let's do that," Kiaan replied with a deep sigh, forcing a smile. Kavya observed everything closely, her heart swelling with a mix of pride and embarrassment. As the ribbons were cut and the ceiling was adorned with balloons, she smiled secretly, revelling in the knowledge that her love for Kiaan had taken over the restaurant that night.

The atmosphere shifted, a strange happiness filling the space. Kavya felt as if she was on a euphoric high. Love is a drug, she thought. She had seen many red carpets in her life, but today she's made the ceiling red—just for the man she adored. As customers started pouring in, a buzz of excitement filled the restaurant. Everyone was captivated by the balloons, and questions swirled in the air about who could have sent such an extravagant gift. "How can someone love like this, not even knowing if they'll get a 'yes'? Spending this much is just madness," one guest commented to a server. The server smiled politely. "Indeed, love has a way of clouding our judgement sometimes." The restaurant was louder than usual, and the mystery of Kiaan's secret admirer became the talk of the evening. Kiaan received praise from customers and his popularity soared beyond normal.

Meanwhile, Kavya was reminded of her desire to work alongside him, not just as a dishwasher, but as someone who could be his right-hand chef. She longed for the day when she could cook next to him, rather than being the nameless girl he occasionally acknowledged. As the night progressed, she yearned to sit with him, talk to him, and even kiss his face. The evening wrapped up smoothly, and Kiaan called for a meeting. "All right, everyone! What a fantastic night it was! Thanks to my mysterious lover, our customers loved the theme tonight. Maybe we should start doing this ourselves more often," he clapped his hands, prompting everyone to join in the applause.

"Have a great night, my amazing team. Now, let me go home and try to figure out who this crazy lover is. Great work tonight, Kavya... you're improving every day!" Kiaan finished, giving her a warm smile. Kavya beamed, feeling a surge of pride as she took off her hair covering, letting her hair fall over her shoulders. Kiaan glanced at her, and for a brief moment, their eyes met.

"Can I drop you off home, K?" Kiaan asked, his voice casual. "No, it's okay. I just need to go to the train station," she replied, trying to hide her excitement. "Well, I can drive you to the train station if you'd like," he offered, his tone sincere.

She knew she must be smelling like sweat after working hard all night, but the prospect of being close to him was too tempting to resist. "Okay," she agreed, her heart racing. "Alright, let's go," Kiaan said, and they both walked under the canopy of red balloons she created, a silent testament to her feelings. They climbed into Kiaan's SUV, and the air was thick with unspoken words. The air conditioning hummed, but Kavya could feel the heat rising beneath her shirt as she sat next to him. She longed to tell him how much she loved him, to express the depths of her feelings, but instead, she remained silent, caught in her thoughts. As they arrived at Grand Central Terminal, Kavya unbuckled her seatbelt and turned to Kiaan. "Thank you," she smiled appreciatively. "See you tomorrow at work," he replied, a warm smile gracing his lips as he drove off. Kavya could hardly believe how close she was to him.

Bypassing the train, she called an Uber and headed back to her penthouse. "Hey, doorman. What's your actual name?" she asked, feeling exhausted after her shift.

"Liam, ma'am," the tall man replied, opening the door for her as she juggled a few bags. "Oh, hello! I'm sorry I kept calling you 'doorman.' I didn't know your name," she said, a little embarrassed. The scent of sweat clung to her, and stains of pasta mar her once-white shirt, making her feel a bit messy. "It's okay. A lot of people don't remember names these days with everything being digital," Liam replied calmly, as he always did. At that moment, Kavya realised how arrogant she had been. Working in the back of the kitchen had humbled her. Right now, her heart was full of love, and she was determined to write a letter to Kiaan—not just any letter, but a token of her love.

The Art Exhibition

"You will make it to the art exhibition on time? It starts at 6:00 pm," Mia texted, her heart fluttering with anticipation. Sitting in her clinic, she could hardly focus on her last client, eager for Kiaan's response. "Oh yes, of course. I should be there right at the dot," Kiaan replied just seconds later, his quick response making her smile.

With a quick breath to steady herself, Mia turned her attention to her next client. "Good evening, Ms. Julia. Thank you for coming in today for your consultation about the facelift procedure. How are you feeling?" Mia greeted warmly. "Good evening, Doctor. I'm a bit nervous but also excited about the possibility of rejuvenating my appearance. You know, at the age of 50, you start to lose your charm," Julia replied, a hint of anxiety in her voice. Mia nodded understandingly.

"Yes, I understand. This is New York, after all. It's completely normal to have mixed feelings before such a procedure. Can you tell me about the specific concerns you have regarding your face that you'd like to address?" Julia took a deep breath. "Well, I've noticed my skin has started to sag, especially around my jawline and cheeks. I also have deep wrinkles that make me look older than I feel." "I completely understand," Mia said, her tone professional yet empathetic. "A facelift can certainly help tighten the skin and smooth out those wrinkles.

During the procedure, we'll remove excess skin and reposition the underlying tissues to create a more youthful appearance. Have you given any thought to what your specific goals or expectations are for the outcome?" Julia smiled softly.

"I just want to look refreshed and natural. I don't want to look like a completely different person—just a better version of myself. You know, like a plastic doll? Men are not attracted to that. The dating world in your 50s is a whole new experience." They both laughed, and Mia felt a warmth in her heart. "Oh, I'm not aware of that.

"I thought life got easier in your 50s—you've seen it all! But that's a reasonable goal, and it's important to have realistic expectations. Rest assured, I will work closely with you to achieve the results you desire. Is there anything else you'd like to discuss before we schedule the procedure?" Julia shook her head.

"No, I think you've answered all my questions. Thank you for taking the time to explain everything to me. Please make me look tempting again like I was in my 40s. The best age for any woman! Men are slaves to you!" Their laughter echoed in the room, dispelling any remaining tension. "Of course, Ms. Julia.

I'm here to guide you through every step of the process and ensure your comfort and satisfaction. Let's go ahead and schedule your facelift procedure. You're in good hands. Please see the receptionist, and she will set your dates."

"Thank you, my love. You are a lifesaver!" Julia exclaimed. "The pleasure is all mine. Let's make you look youthful again. Have a wonderful evening, Julia!" Mia said as she walked Julia to the door, waving goodbye as she headed towards the receptionist. Once back in her office, Mia picked up her phone and called her front desk. "Nita, hun, can you please send me the dress that was delivered from the dry cleaning?" Moments later, Nita brought the dress to her.

Mia placed it on her chair and quickly changed out of her blue scrubs into the sleek black dress. She opened the drawer of her work cabinet, filled with shimmers and glitters, and added a touch of sparkle to her look. With a spritz of perfume and a quick touch-up on her makeup, she grabbed her Hermès purse and headed to her black Range Rover, excitement bubbling within her.

The woman who commands her own life is a force to be reckoned with, and tonight she would shine. Arriving at 11 West 53rd Street, she was relieved to find a parking spot for her Range Rover. Switching her flats for a pair of elegant heels, she glanced in the mirror one last time, adjusting her hair before stepping out of the car.

As she approached the entrance, she presented her ticket to the attendant. It was 7:00 pm. She stepped into the gallery, scanning the crowd for Kiaan but finding no sign of him. A flicker of curiosity ignited in her mind—would he surprise her by showing up?

Just then, a mischievous thought crossed her mind: Did he even know anything about art? A playboy, a chef—that was all she knew about him. Suddenly, a familiar voice broke her thoughts. "Hello!" Kiaan greeted, tapping her shoulder from behind. He looked dapper in corduroy pants, a crisp cotton white shirt, and a luxurious dark blue velvet jacket. "Oh hey! You made it!" she said, turning to smile at him.

Kiaan leaned in for a hug, and she hesitated for a moment before wrapping her arms around him, allowing the moment to linger before pulling away. "Of course! I love art," Kiaan replied, his dimples deepening, making her heart flutter.

They moved through the first exhibit, a server offering them glasses of champagne. They accepted, clinking their glasses together as the sound echoed in the air. "Do you know the tradition behind the cheers?" Kiaan asked, a playful glint in his eye. Mia shook her head, her attention still captivated by the art.

"Well, historically, when two rivals met, they would clink their glasses. If there was poison, it would splash over to the other glass. That's why they would clink harder," he explained, sipping from his glass. "Okay," she said, clinking her glass against his again, this time with more force. "Sip," she instructed playfully.

Kiaan took a sip, raising an eyebrow. "You know, I didn't mean that literally," he said with a smirk. "Look at this painting," Mia said, shifting the conversation as she gazed at the canvas. They found a bench and sat to admire the artwork.

Kiaan remained silent for a moment, seemingly lost in thought. "You know, I will never understand why these abstract art pieces sell for so much," Mia mused, taking a sip of her champagne and glancing at Kiaan, who still stared intently at the painting.

Just then, he spoke. "It's a Rothko painting. The green and blue colours undulate and glitter, playing mind tricks on you as if you're falling into the canvas. Rothko taps into a primal, instinctual essence." Mia turned to him, surprised. "Let's go to the next one," she suggested, unsure of how to react. "Pretty sweet date? An art gallery—nice pick," Kiaan followed her, a teasing tone in his voice.

"This isn't a date. I thought maybe you would like to join me at an art gallery," she hesitated, feeling a mixture of flattery and confusion. "Oh, it's perfect! Art is a pure expression of all emotions, ultimately becoming love," Kiaan replied, his eyes sparkling with enthusiasm. Mia stood momentarily stunned. "Look at this painting, Mia. Just the right amount of colour is applied delicately, making these patterns vibrant," Kiaan continued, gesturing animatedly. "So coming back to your question about why abstract art is so expensive? I mean, you can Google it, but in my opinion, it's about the ability of a painting to capture your attention, to make you think about the work put into it—the colours, the thought process, the inspiration, the time taken, and all the emotions involved. It's as if the painting is alive and talking to us," Kiaan expressed, his passion evident.

"Deep thoughts. Are you trying to impress me?" she asked, gazing at him with a mix of scepticism and intrigue. "Maybe a little, but I'm also an artist—a chef, so technically, art is my speciality," he replied with a charming smile. Mia walked beside him, listening intently, her mind racing. How was this possible? She hadn't expected such depth from him. Was it possible he had read about the artists before arriving? The more she interacted with him, the more questions she had. Just then, her phone vibrated in her pocket.

"Oh no, my parking is about to expire. We should head out," she said, showing Kiaan the notification. "You can extend the parking. You know, I've never had someone to go to an art gallery with and then go for drinks afterwards," Kiaan suggested, his eyes hopeful.

Mia hesitated, caught in a silly game with her sister Kavya and feeling exhausted. "No, I think I want to go home. I'm a bit tired," she replied, wishing for a way out. "Party pooper," he teased, a playful smirk on his face. "Well, not really. I'm just really tired," she rolled her eyes, trying to maintain her resolve.

"Sure, I'm just kidding. We can go for drinks another time," Kiaan said, his tone lightening. She smiled back at him, feeling a flicker of relief. "Let's see the last exhibit and then call it a night," she said, turning to walk towards the next room. "Sure, if that's what you want," Kiaan replied, walking alongside her, both of them immersed in the vibrant world of art. As they strolled through the gallery, Mia felt a mixture of excitement and uncertainty. Tonight had turned out to be more than she had anticipated, and as much as she tried to keep her guard up, she couldn't help but wonder where this unexpected connection might lead. She was definitely leaning towards Kiaan.

India Traffic

The apron Kavya wore did little to shield her from the splatters and stains that seemed to accumulate on her shirt as she navigated through the bustling kitchen. The deodorant she had applied that morning had faded away, mingling with the unfamiliar scent of sweat that lingered on her skin. She had never experienced such a smell while working out in her personal gym back in India, and now, standing in a crowded subway train, she felt acutely self-conscious.

Was the sweat from working out really that different from the sweat of working in a hot kitchen? As she stood there, lost in thought, she glanced around the subway car. Everyone seemed glued to their phones, and Kavya couldn't help but pull out her own device. With over a million followers on Instagram, she had become accustomed to the virtual world, but today it felt empty. She clicked on her notifications and was greeted by a flood of likes—8,000 to be exact.

Her heart sank a little as she scrolled through the hearts and comments, each one a reminder of the admiration she received online but still longing for the one heart that truly mattered—Kiaan's. She wished she could post a picture tagging his restaurant, but that would reveal her true role: a kitchen helper rather than the glamorous celebrity everyone thought she was.

Her eyes wandered over her recent photos, and tears pricked at her eyelids. Just a few weeks ago, she had been on a private island in Italy, indulging in the luxury her father's black card afforded her.

How she missed that life! She glanced down at her clothes—simple, functional, and utterly unremarkable compared to the designer outfits she was used to. But she reminded herself that love could move mountains—she was willing to sacrifice for the chance to be with Kiaan.

As she stood in the crowd of the subway train, she felt like a ghost. One of India's top celebrities is now just another face in New York City, a city that didn't care about her fame. The train jolted to a stop, snapping her out of her reverie.

This was her station, conveniently located next to a grocery store. She would need to take an Uber home after this, as her building was a couple of blocks away. Thankfully, her shift had ended early, and she would be home before Kiaan, who didn't need her today since the restaurant was slow. As she stepped onto the platform, a spark of inspiration ignited in her mind. Tonight, she would cook a special dinner, hoping to impress Kiaan. She recalled the saying she had heard in movies: the way to a man's heart is through his stomach.

Mia had taken care of all her needs since she arrived in New York, and this would be her first time stepping into a grocery store. Back in India, her mother had an entire staff dedicated to the kitchen, including a personal chef.

Kavya wouldn't even know how to boil an egg if asked, but love had pushed her to take this dare. As she walked through the grocery store, it felt like a museum to her. Rows upon rows of products lined the shelves, each one looking foreign and strange, like a forest of food. She turned her cart into an aisle and picked up an item, squinting to read the label.

"Cheese," she read aloud, picking up a pack and flipping it over to examine the back. But before she could shop any further, she realised she would need a recipe. Kavya pulled out her phone and Googled "easy dinner recipes". After scrolling through the results, she clicked on a pasta and meatballs recipe and took a screenshot.

One thing was sorted; she now knew what she would cook.

A smile crept onto her face as she thought about Mia's shocked expression. All she needed now was pasta sauce, onions, meatballs, and Parmesan cheese. With determination, Kavya surveyed the towering shelves filled with cheese and laughed at the absurdity of it all. Her feet were starting to ache, and finding these ingredients felt like searching for a needle in a haystack.

But when faced with a problem, did you cry or laugh? Kavya chose to laugh; it always made the problem seem smaller. Suddenly, a voice broke through her thoughts.

"Hello, miss. Could you move your cart?" A tall Caucasian man, broad-shouldered and imposing, stood beside her, waiting impatiently. Kavya, taken aback, replied defensively, "Excuse me?" "You know this isn't India's traffic where you can park anywhere. There are other people who want to shop too," the man huffed as he brushed past her. Kavya remained silent, her cheeks flushing with indignation.

"I'm quite aware this is America. Unfortunately, I've never been in a grocery store before," she explained, trying to stay polite despite her annoyance. "Yeah, alright, Karen," he muttered as he turned into the next aisle, leaving Kavya bewildered.

"I am Kavya. I think you're mistaking me for someone else," she said. She had no idea that "Karen" was a term used to describe entitled people who create trouble. There was no dictionary she could consult at this moment. Determined to find her ingredients, Kavya scratched her head and looked at her phone once more.

"Okay. Where the hell is this Parmesan cheese?" "Miss, can I help you with something?" A young man dressed in a white shirt and black pants, his Whole Foods name tag reading "Tyler," approached her with a friendly smile. "Can you please help me find these ingredients?" Kavya asked, feeling completely out of her element. "Of course! I can walk you to all of them if you like. The Parmesan cheese is in aisle 1, meatballs are in the frozen aisle 15, pasta and sauce are in aisle 11, and onions are in produce," he said, guiding her with a cheerful demeanour.

"Can you please walk me to all of those?" Kavya requested, grateful for the assistance. "Sure!" Tyler led her through the store, stopping first at the cheese aisle.

"Here's the Parmesan cheese. We also have it in another aisle if you're looking for the dry type," he explained. "Which one is better?" she asked, tilting her head in curiosity. "The fresh one is a little pricier, but it tastes better. The other one is cheaper, and they both have slightly different flavours," he replied.

"Okay, I'll take the fresh one," she decided, placing it in her basket. "Thank you!" she said, feeling a surge of relief. They continued through the aisles, and Kavya carefully selected the rest of her ingredients, placing them in her basket. "Is there anything else I can help you with, miss?" Tyler asked as they reached the checkout area.

"No, I think this is good for now. Thank you!" she replied, her voice filled with gratitude. "It looks like you're making pasta with meatballs?" he observed. "Yes! I'm trying to impress my cousin," she said, a proud smile spreading across her face as she held her grocery basket, which felt heavier with each passing moment. "I think you should get some garlic bread to go with that meal. It would be perfect," he suggested, his smile genuine.

"Sure, let's do that!" Tyler led her to the bakery section and gently placed a loaf of garlic bread in her basket. "Thank you so much for helping me out. I had no idea where everything would have been. This is my first time making pasta," she admitted, feeling both excited and nervous. "Well, good luck! Have a great day," Tyler said as he waved Mia goodbye, leaving her to pay for her groceries.

Kavya gathered her bags and ordered an Uber, feeling a sense of accomplishment. "Where to?" the driver asked as she settled into the back seat. "…add the address to the penthouse," she replied, excitement bubbling inside her. "Okay," the driver acknowledged as they pulled away from the kerb. The ride was quick, and soon she found herself standing outside her building. With one bag in her hands, she made her way to the entrance, where Liam, the doorman, held the door open for her. "Ma'am, please give me the bags, and I will carry them for you," Liam offered politely. "Sure, thank you, doorman… I mean Liam," she corrected herself, feeling a twinge of embarrassment. "You're welcome," he replied, taking the bags from her as they walked to the elevator together. In the elevator, an awkward silence enveloped them. Finally, Kavya broke the tension. "Sorry," she said, glancing at him. "For what?" Liam asked, confused.

"You know, for always calling you doorman instead of your name?" she explained, her cheeks warming.

"Oh no, it's fine. I never thought anything of it," he assured her, brushing it off. Kavya let the moment wash away, grateful for his easygoing nature. "Okay, thank you," she said softly, feeling relieved.

Ding! The elevator chimed as they reached her floor. The silence had been daunting, but she didn't want to say anything else that might lead to further awkwardness. Liam carried her bags to her penthouse, and she pointed towards the kitchen, "In the kitchen. I'm cooking today." He nodded and walked into the kitchen, placing the bags on the counter. "Thank you," she said, feeling a warm sense of gratitude. “You’re welcome,” Liam replied, stepping back towards the elevator. As the door closed behind him, Kavya took a deep breath and looked around her spacious kitchen. It was time to put her plan into action and whip up a meal that would hopefully impress Kiaan.

She couldn’t help but feel a mixture of excitement and nervousness as she prepared to embark on this culinary adventure for the first time.

Cooking for Who?

The grocery bags lay scattered on the kitchen floor, remnants of Kavya's ambitious plans. Exhausted and feeling grimy, she made her way upstairs to her high-ceilinged bedroom, her mind still replaying the encounter with the rude man in the grocery store.

She had felt so out of place, so vulnerable, and the sting of his words lingered like a bad aftertaste. Determined to shake off the day's frustrations, she peeled off her clothes and stepped into the shower. As the warm water cascaded over her, she lathered her hair with shampoo, letting the soothing liquid wash away the stress of the day.

The warmth enveloped her like a much-needed hug, a comfort she desperately craved. She thought about how she might have treated Liam, the doorman, in a similar manner, taking his patience for granted. What was wrong with parking her grocery cart in the aisle? It wasn't like it was a busy road.

It was a grocery store, a place where people should be able to move freely, and she should be able to shop without feeling judged. The water splashed around her, but her thoughts continued to swirl, each one more tangled than the last. After rinsing off, Kavya dried herself and slipped into a white satin silk night suit that felt luxurious against her skin. She was determined to surprise Mia, who would be home in about an hour.

With a smile tugging at her lips, she walked downstairs, her heart fluttering with excitement. In the kitchen, she spotted the scattered groceries—the onions, pasta, sauce, and meatballs—still lying on the floor. She quickly picked them up, placing each item on the counter, her mind racing as she pulled out her phone to Google the recipe again.

"Dice onions into small pieces. Boil the pasta," she read aloud, her brow furrowing as she scanned the unfamiliar utensils. Never having entered a kitchen before, Kavya felt like an explorer in a foreign land.

But she could do this; she had to learn to cook for Kiaan. The thought of him filled her heart with determination. Feeling an adrenaline rush, she turned on some lively music, letting the beat fill the kitchen with energy. This was her moment—no designer purse or luxury purchase had ever given her this kind of happiness.

She could do this. Kavya found a pot and filled it with water, placing it on the stove to boil for the pasta. As she washed the onions, she took a moment to breathe, then began to chop them into small pieces.

The struggle was real; her knife skills were comically inadequate, and she was grateful no one was watching her fumbling attempts. Just then, the front door creaked open, and Mia entered, dropping her keys on the designated table with a clatter.

"You're in the kitchen, Kavya?" Mia asked, surprise evident in her voice as she walked towards the kitchen. It was a rare sight to see her cousin preparing a meal in the house, especially considering how little she had done so since moving in.

"Oh, hello! Yes, I'm indeed in the kitchen. You should go take a shower; I'll have dinner ready by the time you're done," Kavya replied, feeling a surge of pride as she stirred the pasta in the pot. Mia's mind reeled as she slowly ascended the staircase, disbelief washing over her. What was happening? Meanwhile, Kavya heated oil in a pan and, in a moment of distraction, added the diced onions. As the oil sizzled, it splashed hot droplets onto her arm, causing her to yelp in surprise.

"Ah!" she screamed, dropping the bowl of onions as she instinctively recoiled. The bowl shattered on the floor, and she stood there, stunned and in pain. Mia hadn't even made it halfway up the staircase when she heard the commotion and dashed back into the kitchen.

"What happened?" she exclaimed, noticing Kavya's arm with minor oil splashes. Kavya winced as Mia led her to the sink, running cold water over her arm.

"It's just a little burn," she said, trying to downplay the situation, but her face told a different story. Mia quickly reached for the first aid cabinet in the kitchen, grabbing some antibacterial ointment. "Hold still," she instructed, applying it gently to Kavya's arm.

"Okay, now go sit down, and I'll get you an ice pack," she said firmly. Kavya complied, taking a seat at the kitchen table as Mia wrapped an ice pack in a kitchen towel and placed it on Kavya's arm. "So…," Mia began, her brow raised in curiosity. "You mean dinner?" Kavya replied, raising her shoulders in a mock shrug, trying to lighten the mood. Mia burst into laughter.

"I don't care about dinner! It's you we're looking after. The dishes can wait. Let's focus on you," she said, still chuckling as she held Kavya's arm. "I just wanted to cook for us," Kavya admitted, disappointment creeping into her voice. "Well, we can still cook together, or I can order food. Just one thing though… I'm equally good in the kitchen as you are!" They both laughed, the tension dissipating as they moved back into the kitchen. Half an hour later, the two cousins set the dining table together, placing bowls of steaming meatballs and spaghetti in the centre.

"Oh, wait! I forgot the Parmesan!" Kavya exclaimed, rushing back to the fridge. She retrieved the cheese, grating some over Mia's bowl before sprinkling some on her own.

Finally, they sat down at the dining table, anticipation buzzing in the air. With smiles on their faces, they took their first bites, only to immediately regret it. They both spat out the mouthfuls, their expressions morphing from excitement to horror.

"Oh God, the salt is too much!" Mia exclaimed, wiping her mouth with a cloth napkin. "The noodles melted into the tomato sauce. Yuck!" Kavya chimed in, her face scrunching in distaste as she tried to cleanse her palate with a glass of water.

"I guess it's takeout," they both laughed, the sound echoing in the kitchen as they cleared the table and moved the dishes to the sink.

"The challenge is still on, Mia," Kavya said, her smile returning, a spark of determination in her eyes. "Kavya, you're being really naive. What if Kiaan actually fell in love with me?"

Mia teased, her playful smirk evident. "He won't. Don't worry," Kavya said, a hint of seriousness in her tone as she avoided making eye contact with Mia.

"Good night. I'm going to sleep. Thank you for dinner… you're the best cousin in the whole world," Kavya said, her voice filled with warmth as she hugged Mia tightly. "You're welcome. Sweet dreams!" Mia replied, watching her cousin disappear down the hallway, both of them feeling lighter after sharing the evening together, even if the dinner hadn't quite turned out as planned.

I Can't, I am sorry

"Hello, hello again!" Kiaan exclaimed, appearing behind Mia as she stepped out of a boutique in the bustling mall.

Mia turned, her blue baggy jeans and white crop top catching the late afternoon light. Her hair was casually tied up in a messy bun, giving her a relaxed, effortless look.

She had a brown leather bag slung over her shoulder, and her glasses rested atop her head, nestled in her tousled hair. "Are you chasing me?" she teased, raising an eyebrow, a playful smile on her lips. Kiaan chuckled; there was a hint of mischief in his eyes.

"I am not chasing you. In fact, I was here to see a friend," he replied, though the glint in his gaze suggested otherwise. "Oh, that's great. One of your servers or a client?" Mia probed; her curiosity piqued.

Kiaan grinned, his expression turning slightly sheepish. "Well, hello, interviewer… Fine, I am chasing you. I followed you from your home… Oh no, I don't know where you live… So, I followed you from your work… Oh, no, I don't know where that is either." He chuckled, clearly enjoying the banter.

Mia couldn't help but laugh at his flustered honesty. "Oh, right, right. This is such a coincidence. But I really have to go now; I have some work to take care of," she said, turning slightly to leave, sensing a hint of annoyance in Kiaan's tone.

"Okay, well now! I'll have to chase you down for a coffee," Kiaan said, stepping into her path and blocking her way. She paused, caught off guard by his persistence.

Looking into his expressive eyes, she felt a flutter of hesitation. Deep down, she knew Kavya had feelings for this man, and her heart ached for a brief moment at the thought. "Well, I can spare you 30 minutes, I guess," she relented, a smile breaking through her resolve.

"Thank you, your Highness, for your time. May I lead you to the coffee shop?" Kiaan asked, a charming grin spreading across his face as he extended his hand. "You may," she replied, a playful twinkle in her eye. As they walked side by side, Kiaan held the door open for her at the café.

"Thank you for your chivalry. I hope you will always do this for women," she commented, stepping inside. "Yes, I always do and will continue to do so for my wife," he quipped, following her in.

"Excuse me? You have a wife?" Mia replied, her eyes widening in disbelief.

"I meant my future wife," he clarified, his smile broadening. "You know how cheesy that sounds? And you said last time you would never get married?" she teased, her tone light but curious.

"Well, cheesy isn't common anymore, so I thought maybe I should bring it back. Plus, someone made me change my mind," Kiaan replied, a playful glimmer in his eyes as they made their way to a table.

"You seem to have answers for everything," Mia remarked, her interest piqued. "Not really. You and I being in the same place is a bit of a coincidence. Maybe we do need to bring old love back?" He shot back, pulling out a chair for her. Mia opened her palm with a mischievous glint in her eyes, attempting to divert the conversation.

"Do you see a baby bird on my palm?" she asked, her voice playful. Kiaan shook his head, confusion evident on his face. "No, I don't see anything." "Here, hang onto this bird's jacket," she said, playfully touching his palm before urging him to open his hand. Kiaan obliged, his brow furrowing in intrigue.

"Now you see the bird?" she asked again. He shook his head, a hint of annoyance creeping into his tone. "No, I don't see anything." Undeterred, she touched his palm once more. "Okay, hang onto this. It's the bird's pink hat," she told him, her eyes sparkling with mischief. "Do you see the bird now?" she pressed.

"Nope," Kiaan replied, his voice tinged with exasperation. She burst into laughter, unable to contain her amusement. "Well then, why are you hanging onto its jacket and hat?" "Nice game! Where did you find this little trick to fool me?" he laughed, the tension breaking into lightheartedness.

"It's trending on TikTok, silly! I thought I'd try it on you, and hey, it's pretty good!" She clapped her hands in delight, leaning back in her chair. "Oh, watch out! Don't fall," Kiaan said, placing a supportive hand on her back. She smiled at the gesture, feeling a warmth spread through her. "So, how do you know so much about art?" she asked, shifting back to a more serious tone.

"We're jumping conversations here," he replied, feigning a serious expression. "Well, you only have 30 minutes. The coffee is here, and we've already spent

17 minutes playing games," she pointed out, taking a sip of her coffee.

"Well, that's not fair. Now it's my turn to ask a question," he said, leaning forward with interest. "Why do you always rush?" he inquired, genuine curiosity in his eyes. "Well, I have work. Now it's your turn to answer my question," she shot back, her tone playful yet firm.

Kiaan took a moment to gather his thoughts. "I wasn't sure what I wanted to be, so I tried a few things, one of which was getting a degree in arts," he explained, raising his hands as if to emphasise his point. "And you ended up being a chef?" she asked, tilting her head and looking at him inquisitively.

"Actually, I'm taking over my dad's business. I mean, cooking is also a type of art, right?" Kiaan replied, his lips pressed together as he considered his words. Mia glanced at her watch, the minutes slipping away too quickly. "Time's up. I have to go," she said, rising from her seat.

"Come on! You can spare a few more minutes?" he pleaded, looking at her with those irresistible puppy eyes. She shook her head, grabbed her purse and started to walk away.

"So when is the next date?" Kiaan called after her, trying to catch her attention one more time. "Who said this was a date?" Mia winked playfully before exiting the café, her heart swirling with mixed emotions as she stepped back into the bustling mall. The encounter had left her feeling exhilarated and slightly confused, but one thing was for sure—Kiaan was unlike anyone she had ever met.

Maddie's Wedding!

"You made it!" Maddie exclaimed, enveloping Kavya in a warm hug, her wedding dress shimmering under the soft lights.

Kavya stood in her pink beaded bodycon dress, which flattered her curves and sparkled with every movement. "Of course, I would! You're a sweetheart for inviting me," she replied, returning the embrace. "You're just too cocky to actually show up… Just kidding!" Maddie laughed; her eyes bright with excitement.

"Very funny. You sent me a last-minute invite and it was just a text," Kavya shot back, raising an eyebrow. "I know, I'm sorry! But I'm so glad you made it," Madaline said, her smile genuine. Kavya handed her a tiny, elegantly wrapped bag. "What's this?" Maddie asked, curiosity lighting up her face. "Your wedding present," Kavya said with a grin.

"Aww, you are the sweetest client I've ever had! You're the only one I wanted at my wedding," Maddie said, pulling her in for another hug as she accepted the gift. "Thank you for having me. You look absolutely stunning in this gown," Kavya complimented, taking in Maddie's radiant bridal beauty that resembled a scene from a Hollywood movie.

"Okay, let's finish up the hair, Madi," a stylist called, motioning for Maddie to sit down. "Oh yes, of course!" Maddie replied, settling into the chair. Kavya took that as her cue to exit. "I'm going to grab some champagne," she said as she made her way towards the barn. In the rustic charm of the outdoor barn, Kavya wandered alone, feeling a mix of excitement and apprehension.

The beaded dress hugged her curves perfectly, shimmering in the soft glow of the evening light. Her pink Manolo Blahniks clicked against the wooden floor, creating a harmonious melody with each step.

The white Prada purse swung gracefully from her arm, a striking accessory to her ensemble. She placed her empty glass in a nearby planter, glancing around to see if anyone was watching.

"I wish these Manolos weren't biting my toes right now," she thought, wincing slightly. Despite her initial reluctance to attend the wedding, here she was, dressed to the nines. Clutching her purse tightly, she headed towards the bar for a second glass of champagne.

After all, the only pain she preferred was the kind that came from champagne. She grabbed a fresh glass and walked into the barn, now decorated for the wedding. It was empty for the moment, and she realised she had arrived quite early. She contemplated leaving right after the vows, as she didn't know anyone besides Maddie. The barn was strung with warm yellow lights that danced across the wooden beams. Kavya's gaze swept up, and she felt a sense of awe wash over her. Bored, she began counting tables.

"Ten tables with four chairs each?" She took a sip from her glass, watching as the decoration crew put the finishing touches on the venue. "Do you have a question, madam?" a red-haired woman, heavyset and dressed in jeans and a shirt, asked Kavya.

"Oh, I was just counting tables and chairs. Thank you," she replied, a bit embarrassed. "Okay, let me know if you need anything," the woman said, placing a glass centrepiece adorned with purple plastic flowers and delicate yellow butterflies on the table.

"Are you setting up more tables?" Kavya inquired, intrigued. "No, ma'am. This is a gathering for only 50 guests," she informed her. "That's it? That's strange," Kavya expressed, surprised.

"Most weddings consist of 50 to 60 people, ma'am," the woman explained as she continued arranging the flowers. Kavya stood there, watching her work. "I know. Indian weddings are insane. I saw that huge wedding recently in India where a lot of Hollywood celebrities attended. Even Kim Kardashian was there!" she mentioned, recalling the extravagant event. "You went to that wedding?" the woman exclaimed, her eyes wide with admiration.

"Yeah, it was definitely one of a kind. It felt like stars flooded the streets of Mumbai," Kavya said, taking another sip of her champagne. "Nice! Can I get you another glass?" the woman offered.

"I think two is good for now," Kavya smiled, shaking her head gently. "Okay, enjoy your evening!" the woman replied, and they exchanged smiles before Kavya walked outside the barn. As she stepped outside, she noticed a crowd had gathered.

The venue for the vows was set up on the grass opposite the barn, and guests were arriving in their elegant attire. Men donned suits and jackets while women wore colourful dresses, with only the bride expected to wear white. She watched as the tables and chairs began to fill, and soon, the groom and his groomsmen entered the venue, all dressed sharply in black and white. Kavya found her seat, the music playing softly in the background as guests chatted and settled down. She sat in the back row, hoping to remain inconspicuous. Her heart raced as she observed the groom, looking dapper in his suit, and her eyes scanned the other groomsmen.

Suddenly, her heart dropped—Kiaan was among them. Before she could process the situation or find a way to escape, the bride walked in with her father, and everyone stood in respect. Kavya felt trapped. Kiaan might not recognise her in this glamorous outfit, but if she got up to leave, he would undoubtedly see her.

She sat still, hoping Kiaan wouldn't notice her. But as he stood there among the groomsmen, his eyes caught hers for a brief moment, and a look of surprise crossed his face. They exchanged smiles, a silent acknowledgement of their connection.

As the ceremony continued, Kavya's anxiety grew. "You may kiss the bride," the priest announced, and the crowd erupted into applause as the couple was pronounced husband and wife. Everyone stood and followed the newlyweds into the barn, where the reception awaited. Kavya took a deep breath, preparing herself for an awkward encounter.

"Hello!" Kiaan said, catching her just as she was trying to blend into the crowd. "You look stunning.

I never thought I had such a hot staff," he added, his gaze sweeping over her from head to toe. "Oh, thank you! It's all thanks to a dear friend who lent me her outfit, purse, and shoes," she lied, feeling a bead of sweat trickle down her back from nerves. "Well, that's very nice of her," Kiaan replied, his smile genuine.

"Sorry, Kiaan, but I really have to leave now," Kavya said, glancing towards the exit. "Oh Lord, I must be a woman repellent," he laughed, though his eyes betrayed a hint of disappointment. "Why would you say that? I notice how all the women are always around you," she said with a playful smile, trying to lighten the mood.

"Oh, those are just my servers. We've worked together for a long time, and when new ones come in, they blend in with my old crew," Kiaan explained, his expression softening. "Oh," she replied, her heart sinking slightly. "But I did repel someone special," he added, a hint of sorrow in his voice.

"Oh," she echoed, feeling her heart race. He was supposed to be in love with her! "I think I'm in love with someone," he confessed, looking away for a moment. "Oh," Kavya responded, her expression blank as she struggled to hide her disappointment.

"I don't know why I'm telling you this, but you're the sweetest," Kiaan said again, his gaze sincere. Kavya stood there, her mind racing as she tried to figure out who this mystery woman could be. Her heart pounded in her chest. "You were leaving, right? I won't hold you back," Kiaan said, stepping back slightly. "I came early, so I could leave early," she told him, feeling the weight of the moment.

"Okay. Well! It's good to see you!" he said, opening his arms. Kavya wanted to linger in the embrace, but Kiaan let her go too soon. She took a deep breath as she exited the venue, slipping into her BMW. She hoped he wouldn't notice her leaving in such a luxurious car. She could borrow clothes, but she couldn't borrow a Beamer. As she drove away, her heart felt heavy with the realisation that her feelings for Kiaan were complicated, tangled in a web of unspoken emotions and missed opportunities.

The Cartoons

"Oh, look at you in that red sweater and blue jeans!" Kiaan exclaimed, glancing over at Mia as they drove along the highway in his car.

"Is that a compliment?" Mia raised an eyebrow, a playful smile spreading across her face. "Absolutely, and very vintage," Kiaan replied, casually dressed in jeans and a shirt, topped with a stylish jacket.

The evening air was a bit chilly, and soft background music played from the car's speakers. "Thank you," she said, tucking a loose strand of hair behind her ear. "Thanks for coming out with me. I really wanted to show you this cool spot," Kiaan said as he focused on the road ahead. "You're welcome. It was convincing; I usually don't have much free time," she admitted, her smile genuine. A comfortable silence settled between them for a moment.

“So, do you really work seven days a week?” Mia broke the silence, her curiosity evident. “I do,” Kiaan replied, tilting his head slightly, his smile warm. Mia couldn’t help but admire that smile. A part of her longed to lean closer and kiss him, but she reminded herself that this was a game she was trying to navigate. With a sigh, she shook off the thought. “When do you find time for yourself?” she pressed on. “Oh, I make my own ‘me time’ whenever I want. My staff is pretty good, except for one… but she’s new,” he said, raising an eyebrow.

“Oh really? What’s up with her?” Mia asked, intrigued. “I’m not sure; it just seems like she’s never lifted a plate in her life. I bumped into her at a wedding this past weekend, and she didn’t look like someone who belonged in the kitchen,” Kiaan shared, a hint of suspicion colouring his tone.

He parked the car in a beachfront lot, and Mia remained silent, knowing she was the one who had helped Kavya pick out a dress for that very wedding.

“Wow, where are we?” Mia asked, her eyes widening as she took in the view of the water. “Paradise, close to my place,” Kiaan said with a smile. “I didn’t think you’d like a place like this,” she remarked, glancing at him curiously. “And why is that?” Kiaan asked, his interest piqued. “Well, with that muscular build, those tattoos on your biceps, your hairstyle, and the fact that you work with hot waitresses…" she trailed off, raising an eyebrow playfully.

"Oh, so you're stereotyping me? Are you going to say I'm also a cokehead?" Kiaan chuckled, but his phone buzzed, and he checked the notification from Uber. "Have you?" Mia asked, her eyes narrowing.

"You mean, if I've done coke?" he replied, looking amused. "Yes," she pressed, raising her eyebrows. "Never. Never have, and never will. How about you?" he shot back, glancing at his phone. "Never ever, and never ever will I," she assured him, turning her gaze back to the stunning view. "Oh hey, our food is here!" Kiaan announced, stepping out of the car into the cool breeze.

"You got Uber delivery? Wow. What else are you going to show me tonight? The ocean, the sunset, and now food?" she teased, her smile widening. Kiaan returned to the car with the food and handed her a box. "This is also part of my 'me time,' answering your earlier question," he said, taking a bite of sushi. "Oh. This is magic! How did you find this spot?" Mia marvelled, genuinely impressed. "Just a lot of driving, I guess," he shrugged, a modest smile on his face. "You've probably brought a lot of women here; it's so romantic," she remarked, running her fingers through her hair. "You're the first one," he corrected her. "It's my 'me time' spot. Remember?" "So, you come here often?" she asked, intrigued. "I do. It's a sweet escape. You grab your food, turn up the music, and enjoy the view. The best part? No closing time; you can stay until sunrise," Kiaan said, his eyes sparkling with enthusiasm.

"You have multiple personalities," she teased, her smile playful. "How can you know me so well after just a few meetings?" he questioned. "I know you more than you think," she replied with a quirky smile. "And I don't know you at all. Are you a sales rep? A doctor? Or a serial killer?" Kiaan laughed.

"Why would I be a serial killer?" Mia asked, putting her sushi down. "Why not? Some woman walks into my restaurant and asks me out for drinks, and I agree to it," he chuckled. "Oh, please, we're not living in the age of chivalry. It's all about equality now; we all make money, and we all have the same rights," she shot back. "I still want to open the door for my woman, lift her in my arms, and carry her inside. It's just being a gentleman," Kiaan insisted.

"Wow, sophistication? Where is this man when I'm in the restaurant?" she smiled, genuinely curious. "What sort of man are we talking about? I'm just a chef there; that's it," he replied. "You know, the one who's always surrounded by hot waitresses?" she teased. "Are you jealous?" he asked playfully, raising an eyebrow with a grin. "Sounds like you might have some feelings for me!" "Please. I will never have feelings for anyone," Mia replied, rolling her eyes.

"And why is that?" Kiaan pressed, genuinely interested. "Because it comes with a marriage package. Getting married should definitely be eliminated," she stated matter-of-factly, taking another bite of sushi. "And why do you think that?" he inquired.

"Because there are really only two sets of happy people in the world: married men and single women. Married men have everything taken care of for them while single women don't have to do anything," she explained, laughing heartily. "That's a funny statement, but it doesn't cover all the facts," Kiaan countered, his tone thoughtful.

"I know so many married women," she said, shaking her head. "They maintain themselves while juggling the house, jobs, and kids, while men? They do one job and then sit on the couch watching TV." "Hmmm," Kiaan nodded, listening quietly as he considered her words. "They should be helping equally. Why can't one make dinner while the other does the dishes?" she questioned.

"Well, let's cool this conversation down a bit. We have dessert after this," he said with a smile. "I can't believe you prepared all this; it's so cute," she said, her heart warming. "It's a date, right? I have to impress this gorgeous woman," he replied, his gaze earnest. "No, it isn't a date. We're just hanging out," she corrected him, taking another bite and glancing away. "Sure, we're just hanging out," he echoed, pulling out two containers that were a vibrant purple.

"What's this?" she asked, taking her container and removing the plastic lid. "Oh wow, this looks beautiful! A purple dessert?" She dug her spoon into the container. "It's a Filipino dessert called halo-halo. Just mix it all together and take a bite," he explained, mixing his own dessert. "Oh dear goodness, this is like a little piece of heaven on earth," Mia said, closing her eyes as she savoured a bite.

As the sun began to set, the ocean transformed into a canvas of oranges and pinks, reflecting the dying light. "Looks like the sun spilt its sunshine into the ocean," Mia remarked, gazing at the breathtaking view. "So, who are you really? You always seem to be rushing away from me," Kiaan asked, his voice sincere.

"Hey, meet me. I'm Thumbelina," she said playfully, placing her chin on her hand. Kiaan chuckled. "Then I'm Batman," he replied, a grin spreading across his face. "We don't need to know each other; you can be Batman, and I'll be Thumbelina," she teased.

"That's not a match for being in love. Batman is a man, and Thumbelina is a fairy who lives in flowers," he pointed out. "We can't be in love, Kiaan. Okay, I like you as a friend. That's why I'm saying let's go for drinks. I wasn't looking for anything more," she clarified, focusing back on her dessert. "Oh, so you probably do this a lot with other men, do you?" Kiaan teased. "No, I don't. I truly don't have the time. Are you kidding me?" Mia replied, gripping her dessert cup tightly. "I'm sorry, but I've taken you to my favourite spot, showed up at the art gallery, and invited you for drinks… and look at this? You agreed to come along for this long drive. I really like you, Mia," Kiaan said, leaning in slightly, as though about to kiss her. "No, sorry. I can't, Kiaan. You know, we're just friends," she pulled back, her heart racing. Kiaan let out a deep sigh. "We are not just friends."

"There is no you and I or can there be?" Mia makes it clear. Kiaan sits there in silence.

"Mia. I have never felt like this before. I love you," Kiaan expresses.

"Let's just call it a night. It's getting dark, and I need to go home," Mia suggested, shifting the focus. As he started the engine, soft music filled the air, creating a cocoon of sound around them. They sat together in an uncomfortable silence, the weight of unspoken words hanging heavily between them.

Wrap The Gifts? Not My Forte!

It was 11 am, and the sun gleamed through the city skyline as Kavya made her way to the restaurant, a flutter of excitement coursing through her veins.

Kiaan had asked her to come in early, and she would never say no to the man she was absolutely smitten with. The thought of spending time alone with him, even if it was for shopping, filled her with anticipation.

Shopping was her therapy, and if the stores were open at night, she would likely be there too. "Good morning, K! You're all set to go?" Kiaan greeted her, looking dapper in his tailored blue suit, a crisp white shirt underneath, and a striking red tie that added a pop of colour to his ensemble. Kavya felt her heart race.

It had been over a month since she started working at the restaurant, and each day had felt like an uphill battle. Her fingertips bore the evidence of her hard work, adorned with a patchwork of cuts and scrapes. "Yes, I am very ready!" she beamed, her enthusiasm barely contained.

This was a moment she had been waiting for—just her and Kiaan, alone in the car. It felt like a date to her, even if she hadn't yet confessed her feelings. As she turned to walk towards the truck, she accidentally bumped into a pole, causing a glass bottle filled with oil to slip from her grasp and shatter on the floor.

Distracted by Kiaan's handsome presence, she couldn't help but smile at her own clumsiness as butterflies fluttered in her stomach. Kavya followed Kiaan to his sleek black Ram truck, her heart pounding in anticipation.

"Alright, let's get in and go. I'll explain the task as we drive to the mall," Kiaan said as they climbed into the vehicle. The engine roared to life, and as they navigated the bustling streets of New York, Kavya felt a mix of exhilaration and anxiety. The air felt thick with anticipation, her mouth dry, and sweat pooling at her back.

Each bump in the road sent a jolt of nervous energy coursing through her. She had never imagined she would be alone with him like this, and the intimacy of the moment was both electrifying and terrifying. "This is a nice day for shopping," Kiaan remarked, glancing out at the cityscape as he drove.

"Thank you for bringing me along," Kavya replied, her voice light. The sun shone brightly, but the chill in the air was invigorating. Kiaan took a sip from his coffee mug, "Of course! You seem smarter than all the other girls I know," he said with a grin.

"That's a bit mean to say," she teased, a mock frown on her face. "It's a compliment," he assured her, his eyes sparkling. "And how exactly do you determine that I'm smart? I'm just a kitchen helper in your restaurant," she challenged, raising an eyebrow.

"Okay, okay, I take it back. You're all smart and beautiful ladies. I'm just lucky to be surrounded by you," Kiaan said, turning sharply as he found a parking spot.

Kavya couldn't believe it; she was finally out of the kitchen and helping him shop. Shopping was a delightful escape for her. "Shouldn't we have gone to Manhattan for shopping?" she suggested, unsure of the city layout. Kiaan burst out laughing.

"This isn't Manhattan; it's more like 'Madhattan'—maybe 20 years ago," he joked as he hopped out of the truck and opened the door for her. Kavya's heart raced at the chivalrous gesture. She was filled with giddy excitement, wanting to jump up and down, but she forced herself to maintain her composure. Men could be unpredictable, and she wanted to present her best self.

As they walked towards the store, the crisp autumn leaves crunched underfoot. The sky was overcast, hinting at the impending snow, but the warmth of being next to Kiaan made her feel cosy. “Let’s get into this store and find gifts for everyone,” Kiaan suggested, leading her into TJ Kiaanx. Inside, the store was filled with the scent of fresh merchandise and the soft hum of chatter.

A comfortable silence enveloped them as they browsed. “You work with all of them. You probably have a better idea of what they’d like,” Kiaan remarked, passing her a decorative piece he thought might suit one of the staff. “I’ve only been with them for a short time, but I’ve seen them around,” Kavya replied, her hesitation evident.

“Maria, Jessi, and Danny are like family. They’ve been with us for a long time. Ronald started as a helper and has been with us for a while now. And John worked with my dad years ago,” he shared, strolling through the aisles with ease. “What about the girls?” Kavya asked, intrigued. “Oh, my dark side, you mean?” Kiaan laughed, a playful glint in his eye. “Dark side?” she echoed, confusion knitting her brow.

"Yes, I have a dark side," he said, biting his lip as he glanced down, then back up at her, a charming dimple appearing on his cheek. Kavya felt a rush of warmth wash over her, her heart racing at the thought of his "dark side". She didn't want to hear anything that could complicate her feelings for him.

As they wandered through the aisles, Kavya absentmindedly picked up a purse, admiring it. "This would be perfect for Maria," she thought, holding it against her body as Kiaan moved further down the aisle. "I'm going to check out a few things in the men's section. Why don't you browse in the girls' section? It'll save us time," Kiaan suggested, moving away. Kavya watched him walk off, her mind racing. What kind of darkness was he referring to?

Her suspicions bubbled up, especially after seeing him with different women at work. The sight of him leaving with two different women on consecutive days made her stomach churn. Just as she was lost in thought, a loud commotion broke her reverie. "Kavya! Kavya!" a group of girls exclaimed, rushing towards her with bright smiles. Kavya was suddenly surrounded by five or six excited fans. "Oh my goodness, it's Kavya!" one girl in her twenties exclaimed, her eyes wide with disbelief. "Kavya, can we please take a selfie?" another girl asked eagerly. Shaking off her unsettling thoughts, Kavya smiled brightly."

"Of course! Let's take a selfie." She stepped into the centre, and they all posed together, laughter filling the air. As they chatted animatedly, Kavya felt a rush of happiness.

"Kavya, you look so beautiful! We're huge fans! It's such a lucky coincidence to meet you here!" one of the girls gushed. "Thank you, that's so kind of you!" Kavya replied, her heart swelling as they waved goodbye and walked away.

Just then, Kiaan walked into the aisle, catching sight of Kavya still waving at her fans. As soon as she noticed him, she lowered her hand, her cheeks flushing. Kiaan approached her, a few items in his hands. "Wow, what was that all about?" he asked, placing the items into his cart. "Oh, just some friends from India who were excited to see me in New York," she replied, avoiding eye contact as her focus shifted back to the shelves.

Kiaan glanced at the time on his watch. "The store is packed. Maybe next year we should shop a little earlier," he suggested, his tone light. Kavya took a deep breath, feeling grateful to be in New York where she could enjoy this kind of attention.

Back in India, bodyguards would have kept fans at a distance. Kiaan glanced at the neatly arranged gifts on the counter, his heart racing with anticipation. "Kavya, could you do me a favour? Please take my credit card and handle the payment for these. And if you don't mind, could you also get them wrapped? I'll pay you for the entire day," Kiaan said, looking at her earnestly.

Kavya paused for a moment, caught off guard by his request. The bustling store around her faded into a blur as she lost herself in thought. She had her own errands to run and her own gifts to purchase, yet Kiaan's request pulled at her like a magnet. "You know what? It's okay if you can't," Kiaan said, a hint of disappointment creeping into his voice. "I'll just ask some other girl to wrap them."

His words pierced through her reverie, igniting a familiar warmth in her cheeks. Why did he have to tease her like this? Her internal dialogue buzzed with confusion and a flicker of annoyance. "Oh no, I will wrap those!" she quickly responded, her voice carrying a mixture of determination and a hint of playfulness.

As she spoke, a smile bloomed on her face, unbidden and bright. Kavya's thoughts tangled up, and she couldn't help but think that Kiaan must know how she felt about him.

The realisation sent a pleasant shiver down her spine, and she couldn't help but smile even wider. "Okay, I'll wrap them," she said again, her tone now more confident as she met Kiaan's gaze. A connection, a bond seemed to shimmer just beneath the surface. She felt a thrill of excitement; perhaps this was the beginning of something more than just friendship. As Kiaan grinned back at her, Kavya's heart danced with hope, igniting a spark of possibility.

As the cashier scanned the presents, she announced, "Ma'am, your total is $1,239." Kavya swiped the credit card that Kiaan had given her, feeling a mix of excitement and anxiety. "Do you think we could get all these wrapped?" Kavya asked the cashier, suddenly realising that she hadn't planned for this.

"Please take them to customer service, and they will have them wrapped and delivered to your house," the cashier instructed, pointing towards the customer service counter.

Kavya took a deep sigh and gathered all the gifts, walking towards the counter. She would do anything for Kiaan, but wrapping presents was not her forte.

As she approached the customer service desk, she felt a blend of nerves and determination.

Today was about more than just shopping; it was about the possibility of something blossoming between her and Kiaan. She just hoped she could keep her feelings in check long enough to enjoy this day with him.

Blood!

"Kavya, take these flowers and put them in all the vases," Maria instructed, handing her a bouquet of fresh white flowers. The restaurant was closed for customers today, preparing for a special Christmas celebration for the staff.

The atmosphere buzzed with excitement as the team decorated the dining area. Tables were draped in crisp white tablecloths, adorned with vibrant red table runners that created a festive contrast. The dimmed lights cast a warm glow throughout the room, enhancing the holiday spirit.

Kavya picked up the flowers and stepped out of the kitchen, navigating through the lively crowd. Laughter and chatter filled the air as people chatted and sipped on wine. With her hair down and dressed in a chic black off-the-shoulder dress that fell above her knees, she felt a mix of confidence and nerves.

Carrying the red and white carnations, she smiled at everyone she passed, hoping to spread some of the joy around her. As she arranged the flowers in the vases, her heart raced every time she caught a glimpse of Kiaan. He was busy in the kitchen, expertly preparing a delicious feast for the team.

Today was not about regular menu items; he had curated a special Greek dinner that would leave everyone raving. The tantalising aroma wafting from the kitchen was nothing short of heavenly, making Kavya's mouth water. Kiaan wore a crisp white shirt, complemented by a green apron that emphasised his strong physique.

She couldn't help but admire him from the corner of her eye as he moved effortlessly between pots and pans.

"Danny, please take the Moussaka and Kleftiko and put them on the buffet table," Kiaan instructed, opening the oven to check on the roast chicken. "Ahh, the smell of rosemary is amazing!" he exclaimed, lifting the lid from a pot of lentil soup and inhaling the fragrant steam. Once he was satisfied with everything, Kiaan removed his apron and placed it neatly on the table.

"All right, everyone! Everything is ready! Let's go see our guests and kick off the party!" he called out, adjusting his tie with a flourish as everyone followed him excitedly.

Kavya took a seat at a table nearby, her heart fluttering with anticipation.

She felt a warm blush creeping up her cheeks as she sat there alone, her mind racing back to the afternoon they had spent together shopping. It had drawn them closer, creating a connection that felt both exhilarating and terrifying. Kiaan reached for her hand, lifting it gently to his lips. "Thank you for helping me wrap the presents," he said, his voice sincere and warm. In that moment, Kavya's mind raced. Did she really help wrap those gifts? Not at all. She had opted for the easy route and had them done by a professional. But as she gazed into Kiaan's eyes, she wished it were true, just to savour this moment a little longer.

The restaurant was alive with laughter and conversations, the atmosphere vibrant and full of holiday cheer. The food was superb, and the presents were distributed. When Kiaan asked Kavya to dance with him, she happily accepted the invitation.

They moved onto the dance floor, surrounded by their coworkers, but Kavya hesitated. She wanted to lean into him, to feel his strong arms around her, but the reality of their boss-employee relationship held her back. As the evening progressed, Kiaan stood at the entrance of the restaurant, bidding farewell to his friends as they prepared to leave. "Son, thank you. You've been amazing all these years, and this dinner you put together for your staff is truly special. God bless you," said Maria, leaning in to press a gentle kiss on his forehead. "Of course. Everyone here is my family," Kiaan replied, hugging her tightly. He then held her arm and walked her to the car door.

As she got in, Kiaan closed the door gently and waved goodbye before turning back to head inside. Just then, a sudden thud echoed in the air, accompanied by the sound of tyres screeching. Kavya's heart dropped as she turned to see Kiaan in front of a car that lurched forward, sending him sprawling onto the pavement. Panic erupted among the staff as they rushed towards him.

'Oh my God! I'm so sorry! Someone call an ambulance!' John shouted, his face pale with shock as he leapt out of the car. Kavya's heart raced, and she sprinted towards Kiaan.

'Get away! Let him breathe!' she yelled, making room for him as she knelt beside him. Blood was pooling around him, crimson staining his shirt as severe cuts marred his forehead.

"Stay still, Kiaan. Help is on the way," she urged, trying to keep her voice steady. Ronald quickly moved to support Kiaan's head, ensuring his neck was aligned as they waited for help to arrive. The wail of sirens soon filled the air, and an ambulance pulled up. Paramedics rushed to Kiaan's side, checking for signs of life. Kavya stood frozen, her heart pounding in her chest, watching helplessly as they assessed his condition.

He lay there, silent and unresponsive, the reality of the situation sinking in like a heavy weight. With urgency, the paramedics brought out a stretcher and carefully lifted Kiaan onto it, transporting him into the ambulance. Kavya stood outside the restaurant, her mind racing, trying to process what had just happened.

As the ambulance doors closed, she caught sight of John, who looked distraught, climbing in to accompany Kiaan. Maria stood nearby, tears streaming down her face as she leaned on Jessi's shoulder for support. The ambulance sped away towards the hospital, leaving Kavya standing in the fading light, her heart heavy with worry. The festive atmosphere had vanished, replaced by an overwhelming sense of dread. All she could think about was Kiaan and the hope that he would be okay.

Hospital

“I am going to the hospital,” Kavya declared firmly, standing resolutely in front of the taxi waiting outside the restaurant. Michael, Danny, and Jessi stood nearby, grappling with the chaos that had just unfolded. “You should go home and rest, Kav. We three will be going to the hospital,” Michael suggested, concern etched on his face.

“I said I’m going too!” Kavya insisted, her voice rising in panic. She had only been at the restaurant for a few weeks, but she couldn’t bear the thought of not being there for Kiaan, especially after what had just happened. She had never told him how deeply she loved him, but love had a way of sneaking up on you when you least expected it. It had happened to her, and she wasn’t about to back down now.

"Okay, fine. Danny, let's take her with us," Michael relented, and they all piled into the taxi. As the taxi sped towards the hospital, Kavya's heart raced. The fluorescent lights flickered overhead as they approached the entrance, casting a sterile glow over the bustling lobby. She stumbled out, her pulse pounding in her ears, and rushed towards the ICU, her mind a whirlwind of worry and dread. The air was thick with tension, and every step felt like it took an eternity. When she reached the ICU door, a nurse looked up from her station and gestured for her to wait. Kavya stood frozen, her breath hitching as she peered through the glass.

Inside, Kiaan lay unconscious on the bed, surrounded by an array of machines beeping rhythmically.

The sight of him like this sent a sharp pang of fear through her chest. Outside the ICU, the three men stood with her, their expressions a mix of concern and disbelief. "That's really nice of you to stay, Kav," Michael said, breaking the silence. "Yes, of course. It's not a problem," she replied, trying to hide the turmoil of emotions swirling inside her.

Two long, agonising hours passed before a nurse finally approached her. "You can go in now, the patient has a fractured right arm. Otherwise, he is fine, we have given him some steroids to ease the pain for now, so he is sleeping," she said gently, her expression softening at the sight of Kavya's distress.

Kavya nodded, her heart racing as she stepped through the door, Michael following closely behind her. The sterile scent of antiseptic filled her nostrils, and she moved closer to Kiaan's bedside. He looked so peaceful despite the chaos surrounding him, and for a moment, she almost convinced herself that everything would be alright.

"He looks okay. Just unconscious," Michael said quietly. "I'm going home, K. Call me if something happens. I have to open the restaurant tomorrow." He looked at Kavya with concern, and she nodded in acknowledgement as he prepared to leave.

Once they were alone, Kavya reached for Kiaan's hand, wrapping her fingers around his, her touch warm against his cold skin. "Kiaan," she whispered, her voice trembling with emotion. "I'm here. You're going to be okay. Just hold on. I love you."

His eyelids fluttered slightly, and for a moment, hope surged within her. But instead of waking, he shifted slightly and murmured, "Mia..." His voice was barely audible, yet it struck Kavya like a blow to the chest. A surge of anger bubbled up within her. How could he be calling for Mia when she was right here? The thought twisted painfully in her gut, and she fought against the wave of emotions threatening to overwhelm her.

"Why Mia?" she whispered, her voice cracking. "I'm right here, Kiaan. It's me, Kavya. I need you to wake up. Please." Tears slipped down her cheeks, falling onto his hand as she squeezed it tighter, willing him to feel her presence. "I love you, Kiaan. Just once, listen to what I'm saying."

Minutes turned into what felt like hours, and Kiaan remained still, drifting in and out of consciousness. Each time he murmured Mia's name, a pang of jealousy and hurt sliced through her, deepening the ache in her heart. Kavya sank into a chair beside his bed, her body refusing to move while her mind spiralled into confusion. One question consumed her: When did Mia come into the picture? She had jokingly asked Mia to make Kiaan fall in love with her, but now it felt like a cruel twist of fate.

Anger bubbled within her, mingling with regret over every second spent washing dishes and dreaming of this moment. All dressed up and with nowhere to go, she couldn't allow herself to shed a tear—her makeup would run. Feeling overwhelmed, Kavya stood abruptly and stormed out of the hospital room, her emotions boiling over.

As she walked down the sterile corridor, she felt a mix of anger and heartbreak. How could Kiaan be so oblivious to her feelings? The thought of him calling for another woman, especially Mia, made her stomach churn. She paused for a moment, taking a deep breath to steady herself. Determined to regain her composure, she pushed through the hospital doors and stepped into the cool evening air.

She needed to clear her mind, and as she walked away from the hospital, she felt the weight of what had just happened settle heavily on her shoulders. The love she felt for Kiaan had become a tangled mess of emotions, and she wasn't sure how to untangle it.

Ditch the Bitch

The taxi ride back home felt like a slow descent into a dark abyss, each passing moment intensifying Kavya's turmoil. Kavya stepped out of the taxi, glancing at her phone—4:00 am stared back at her.

"Great, just great," she muttered to herself, feeling the chill of the night seep into her bones. "Where's Liam? Maybe he's only a daytime guy?" She sighed, wishing she had someone to help her to the penthouse.

"Stupid doorman is never there when I actually need him," she murmured as she kicked the door before pushing through the heavy doors and making her way to the elevator.

The elevator ascended to the penthouse; she felt the alcohol from the party had gone, leaving her with this bad hangover. "Ugh, why did I drink so much? But I could use another drink right now," she groaned, rubbing her temples.

"I can't believe what just happened. Kiaan is in the hospital, and he said Mia's name while he was unconscious. What does that even mean?" Her mind raced, the thoughts colliding like a chaotic storm. "Why was he saying her name? I am in love with him! This is insane!" She again banged her fist against the elevator door, but the sting in her hand made her wince in pain. She entered the penthouse and went up to her room.

Once inside, she collapsed onto her bed, staring up at the lofty ceiling adorned with intricate mouldings.

"This place used to feel like home," she whispered, "but now it feels like a war zone." The walls seemed to close in around her as she struggled to process everything.

"Not once did Mia mention Kiaan. Not once! She could have told me, but no! I had to find out from a guy lying unconscious in the hospital. Why would she keep that from me? I don't understand anything right now."

Kavya sat up, feeling suffocated by the weight of unanswered questions. "I can't stand her. Even for a second," she said to herself, determination creeping into her voice. She grabbed a jacket and slipped on her Jimmy Choo heels.

"Everything sucks right now and Mia is probably snoring in her room," she muttered, shaking her head as she walked to the bar next to the kitchen.

She grabbed a half-full bottle of whisky and stepped outside her building. "Just what I need," she said sarcastically, unscrewing the cap and taking a long sip. "This is going to help me forget. Right?" The warmth of the alcohol spread through her, but the confusion lingered.

"I still can't believe what just happened. I feel so blindsided! Damn it, Mia! You could have told me," she thought as she wandered the streets of New York, the city felt both familiar and foreign.

"Why didn't she say anything? Mia and Kiaan are all I have here," she yelled into the night, her frustration spilling over. The makeup from the party began to smudge on her face as tears threatened to fall.

"This isn't fair!" Kavya finished the bottle, tossing it into a recycling bin with a sense of finality. She plopped down on a bench, shivering in the cold, and pulled out her phone.

"Okay, let's see… I'll just text her."

Mia... you could have told me. Kiaan is in the hospital and he was saying your name while he lay unconscious on the hospital bed in the ICU. Can you explain it to me? I thought you were my cousin, but no... you are a bitch. Her fingers shook as she typed.

"No. I can't send this. Not when I'm drunk. That would be a disaster." Her heart raced as she stared at the screen; she realised she loved Mia too. With a frustrated sigh, she put the phone down on her lap. "Fuck man! I never thought these shoes would be so painful." She wiggled her toes, trying to ease the discomfort, but it didn't help.

"Oh God, it's freezing and I hate everything right now," she said, her voice rising in pitch. Finally, she screamed at the top of her lungs, letting the sound echo through the empty streets. "Why is this happening to me?" she cried out, feeling utterly lost and alone, the weight of the night pressing down on her. "I just want to breathe!"

Kavya got up and started to walk back to her building. The heels were biting her feet. She tried to take them off but tumbled into a ditch. She tried to get back on, but the booze in her body said no!

Puke

A single raindrop splattered against Kavya's cheek, jolting her awake as she lay in a cold, damp ditch beside the building. She squinted against the soft light of dawn breaking over the skyline, her surroundings slowly coming into focus.

"Damn," she muttered, pushing herself upright from the ground, her clothes clinging uncomfortably to her skin. "No one woke me up?" she cried out, the realisation of her situation crashing down on her like a wave. They must think I'm some homeless person passed out in a ditch, she thought bitterly. The streets were beginning to fill with people, their morning routines starting, but the rush hadn't quite begun.

She could hear the distant sounds of commuters and cars, but everything felt muted in her hazy mind. As the light rain began to fall, it morphed from a drizzle into large, cold drops, soaking her further. "These are Jimmy Choo heels! Stop looking at me!" she snapped at a man who stared as she stumbled to her feet, trying to regain her composure. The slick pavement made her unsteady as she staggered back onto the sidewalk, attempting to shake the wrinkles from her dress, but just then, the rain began to pour harder.

"Oh God… my dress!" Panic surged in her chest as she realised the beautiful outfit she had worn to the party was now soaked and clinging to her skin. The alcohol still clouded her thoughts, making her feel lightheaded and disoriented. "This is so stupid," she groaned, frustration bubbling to the surface as the downpour intensified. She started to walk, but the slick pavement betrayed her, and she tumbled forward, landing hard on her knees.

"Great," she muttered, wincing at the sting of the impact. She pushed herself up, trying to ignore the embarrassment and the aching pain in her body. "Excuse me… your knee is bleeding," a passerby said, pointing at her scraped skin. Kavya looked down, noticing the crimson streaks on her knee.

"Thank you," she replied, forcing a smile even as humiliation washed over her. The man moved on, leaving her alone in the rain. Standing there, drenched and vulnerable, tears began to spill from her eyes, mixing with the raindrops.

"Oh Lord, I am a complete mess," she whispered to herself, feeling the weight of her emotions crash down around her. She turned and began the walk back to her building, her heart heavy as the tears fell freely. When she finally arrived at her apartment, the hangover, headache, cold weather, and wet clothes combined to leave her feeling utterly defeated.

Yet, a glimmer of hope emerged when she spotted Liam, her doorman, standing by the door. Taking a deep breath, she walked towards him. "Liam!" she called out, her voice cracking under the strain of her emotions. But before she could reach him, the contents of her stomach surged up. In a moment of sheer mortification, Kavya vomited onto Liam's shirt, her face burning with humiliation.

"Oh God, I'm so sorry!" she cried, her cheeks flushed with embarrassment. Liam's eyes widened in surprise, but he quickly shifted from shock to concern. "Are you alright, miss?" he asked, looking worried but also slightly amused. Kavya stood there, drenched and shaken.

"No, I'm not alright," she replied, tears mingling with the rain on her cheeks. "I'm really not alright." "You will be okay, miss," Liam assured her, gently helping her towards the elevator.

The ride felt like an eternity, the weight of the morning pressing down on her. As the elevator doors opened, Mia heard the sound of the door and got up from the couch, placing her coffee gently on the table as she approached Kavya. Her sister's eyes widened in shock at the sight of her. "Kavya! Are you okay?" Mia asked, worry creeping into her voice.

"Don't talk to me. Just go away," Kavya slurred, pushing Mia's hand aside. "Jeez, you can't even walk! You're completely soaked. Let me help you," Mia said, glancing at the clock and realising she was running late for work. "I don't need your help!" Kavya insisted, shoving her away once more.

"What's wrong with you? It looks like you had too much fun at the party last night," Mia replied, gently guiding Kavya down the hallway to her room. Once inside, Mia helped her into the shower, making sure she didn't slip. The hot water cascaded down, washing away the remnants of her night and the panic that had engulfed her. After a quick rinse, Kavya changed into dry clothes, her movements slow and unsteady. "There you go, my party little sister," Mia said softly, tucking Kavya into bed.

Kavya lay quietly, her mind racing despite her exhaustion. Even in her inebriated state, one question gnawed at her: Why did Kiaan say Mia's name? She wanted to lash out and break things, but instead, she challenged herself to remain composed.

The thought of Kiaan calling for another woman twisted her heart, and she felt a surge of anger mixed with regret. After Mia left, Kavya buried her face in the pillow and cried, eventually succumbing to sleep. A few hours later, Kavya awoke with a start, her pillow damp with tears and drool. It was past noon, and she groggily wrapped herself in her robe before making her way to the kitchen. She brewed a cup of coffee, hoping it would help clear her foggy mind. As she curled up on the couch, she turned on the TV.

The news blared, and she lifted her legs, curling into a ball, feeling small compared to the larger-than-life images on the screen. Her head still pounded as she got up to grab some tablets from the cabinet, hoping to ease the pain.

"Oh no," she muttered, remembering the incident with Liam. She had vomited on him! Wrapping her robe tightly around her, she dashed down to the lobby, her heart racing with anxiety.

"Liam!" she called as she approached the door. He looked up, a warm smile spreading across his face. "Good afternoon, Kavya," he greeted, his demeanour friendly. "I'm so sorry about this morning," she said, her voice softening, embarrassment creeping back. "It's no big deal, miss," Liam replied, still smiling kindly.

"I can fix that with a gift if you'd like?" she offered, hoping to make amends. "It's alright, ma'am. I've already changed my shirt," he assured her. Kavya smiled in relief, but she hesitated, still feeling the need to make things right. The lobby was bustling with people coming and going, the afternoon sun streaming through the glass doors.

"It's okay, madam. It's the thought that counts. I appreciate it; plus you were intoxicated. It's not really your fault," Liam said, trying to reassure her. Kavya listened, her heart warming at his kindness. Just then, a man walked by and stopped at Liam's desk.

"How are you, Liam?" asked George, a man in his 50s dressed in a sharp suit. "I'm fine," Liam replied, glancing over at Kavya. "Did you find out about my mailbox?" George asked. Liam checked the register. "It's already fixed, George," he replied.

"Yes, ma'am. Can I help you?" Liam looked at Kavya in surprise. "I would love it if you could come and shop with me on your day off," Kavya said, her voice hopeful.

"Sure, I have the day off tomorrow," Liam replied without hesitation. "Oh, that was easy," she said, a bright smile lighting up her face. "Let's meet in the building lobby at noon," she suggested, feeling a sense of excitement. "Sure, see you tomorrow," Liam replied, his smile warm and genuine.

"Thank you so much, Liam, for saying yes," she said, turning to walk back towards the elevator, her heart feeling just a little lighter. As she stepped inside, she realised that perhaps today wasn't such a mess after all. There was a glimmer of hope, a possibility for new beginnings, even amidst the chaos of her life.

Shopping

Kavya's phone buzzed insistently, pulling her from thoughts of the previous day. She glanced at the screen and saw a text from Liam: I'm downstairs. Quickly, she grabbed her plush fur jacket, slipping it over her fitted jeans and tall boots. As she made her way through her penthouse, the heels of her boots clicked softly against the polished wooden floor, echoing in the quiet space. Stepping into the lobby, she scanned the area for Liam. Just then, she spotted him by the entrance, and her heart skipped a beat. He looked relaxed and approachable, dressed casually in jeans, a fitted shirt, and boots that complemented his tall frame, a stark contrast to his usual doorman attire.

"Oh wow, you look different!" Kavya exclaimed, a smile breaking across her face as she approached him.

"Hello! Yes, I'm not working today," Liam replied, flashing a grin that revealed his dimples, making him look even more handsome.

"Okay, right. So, shall we?" Kavya asked, gesturing towards the exit with an eagerness that felt electric. "Absolutely," Liam nodded, and they headed towards the parking lot together. The air was crisp, filled with the promise of a beautiful day. Once outside, they approached her sleek BMW. Kavya unlocked the doors and slid into the driver's seat, Liam settling in beside her, adjusting his seatbelt. "Ready for some shopping?" Kavya asked, her excitement bubbling over as she started the engine.

"Definitely! This is a better experience than just getting tips," Liam replied, enthusiasm evident in his voice. Kavya smiled at his response, feeling a rush of warmth. "So, what are you? Some big-shot Indian celebrity?" Liam asked, his playful grin lighting up his face. Kavya tightened her grip on the steering wheel, a mix of amusement and pride washing over her.

"I have over a million followers if that counts," she replied, her tone teasing. Liam's jaw dropped in disbelief, and he slammed his hand on the car dashboard. "Damn! Wow! Let me check it out. What's your handle?"

"RealKavya," she said, a blend of amusement and embarrassment washing over her as she watched him pull out his phone. As Instagram popped up with her account, Liam's eyes widened in disbelief. "I'm sitting next to a celebrity? This is nuts!" he exclaimed, scrolling through her photos. "You've got so many likes! You've travelled to Paris, Australia, Prague, Germany, and almost everywhere! You are so lucky."

Kavya remained quiet, a shy smile creeping onto her face as she soaked in the compliments. "So, what are you buying for me today?" he asked; a mischievous glint in his eye breaking the momentary tension. "Anything you want!" Kavya replied, her enthusiasm infectious as they parked and stepped into the bustling mall.

The lively atmosphere buzzed around them, filled with laughter and the tempting aroma of freshly baked pretzels wafting through the air. "Anything?" Liam raised an eyebrow, playful scepticism dancing in his gaze. "Yes! And then we can grab lunch and drinks afterwards," she said, her excitement bubbling over as they entered the mall. They wandered through the bright, cheerful shops, the vibrant displays inviting them in. As they entered a shoe store, Liam picked up a pair of Jordan shoes and held them up to Kavya, a hopeful smile spreading across his face.

"These," he said, his eyes shining with enthusiasm like a child on Christmas morning. "That's it?" she asked, a mix of surprise and curiosity crossing her features. "I'm okay with these," he replied with a laugh, sitting down to try them on, a sense of contentment washing over him. "You do know you can pick any shoe, right?" Kavya pointed out, pulling out her green Hermès purse to apply some lip gloss.

"Oh yeah... are you trying to be my sugar mama?" he teased, his smile playful.

"No, but it's my way of saying sorry, and it has no price tag," she replied with a wink. "No, I'm okay with these. They're comfortable and easy to walk in when I'm at school," he explained, his determination evident as he walked around in the shoes, a contrast to the weight of his responsibilities.

"You're in school?" Kavya looked at him, genuine surprise lighting up her features. "Yes, I'm doing an online programme for an arts degree," he replied, a hint of pride in his voice. "Wow, and you work as a doorman during the day?" she asked, admiration creeping into her tone.

"Everyone has to work. I guess you've never had a job, huh?" he teased, a warm smile spreading across his face. Kavya laughed, feeling a sense of camaraderie.

"Actually, I've been working in a restaurant for a few months as a kitchen helper." "A kitchen helper?" Liam raised his eyebrows, shock evident on his face. They made their way to the counter where Kavya took out her black no-limit card to pay for the shoes. "I'm in love with the chef at the restaurant. I want to marry him," she said, her voice tinged with emotion. Liam took the shoes and walked alongside her, the weight of their conversation hanging in the air as they headed to a nearby restaurant. "Wow, it's crazy in this mall," Kavya remarked, navigating through the bustling shoppers.

"Kav, why work in the kitchen? You're beautiful and famous. Who wouldn't want to date you?" Liam asked, his tone shifting to something more serious. "I don't know, okay? I think he's in love with my sister," Kavya replied, annoyance creeping into her voice. Just then, a teenage girl approached their table, her eyes sparkling with excitement. "Kavya, I'm a huge fan! Can I please get a picture with you?" she asked eagerly. "Oh, sure!" Kavya said, her bright smile returning as she stood up. The girl handed her phone to Liam. "Can you please take our photo?" she asked, her enthusiasm contagious.

"Sure," Liam replied, standing up to capture the moment. "Thank you so much! You look stunning! Are you going to be in any films soon? We'd love to see you act," the girl gushed, her admiration clear. Kavya smiled warmly, her heart swelling with appreciation. "Thank you! I'm not too sure. Maybe one day?" she said, leaving the door open for future possibilities, a flicker of hope shining in her eyes.

"It's my lucky day! Thanks for the photo!" the girl exclaimed before disappearing into the crowd, leaving both Kavya and Liam in awe. "Wow, you're a big deal! Just show up like a star, and they won't say no," Liam encouraged her, his tone light but supportive.

"It's not that simple. I have competition—my own cousin," Kavya explained, her smile fading slightly as the complexity of her feelings returned. "You mean Miss Mia Das? Yeah, she's tough and has a nice figure," Liam said, his expression shifting to one of understanding.

"Oye, you doorman! She's my cousin!" Kavya lightly smacked his arm, laughter spilling forth as they both found joy in the moment.

"Oh, that's why you were drunk? You were a mess," Liam told her.

She nodded her head in agreement and made a frowning face.

Their connection deepened over food and drinks, laughter echoing in the busy restaurant around them, the warmth of their camaraderie brightening the chilly afternoon.

Text Him or Not?

Mia rummaged through her drawer, her fingers dancing over the soft pink silk cloth that housed her cherished toys. Just like her heels and purses, she had them in all colours—each one a reminder of the pleasure and escapism they provided. The dim light in her walk-in closet cast a warm glow on the array of textures and hues, but her thoughts were elsewhere. She was searching for something to help her unwind, a distraction from the whirlwind of emotions that had engulfed her in the past few days.

"Which one, Tom, George, or Brad?" she mumbled to herself, pulling out a silk scarf that partially covered the hot pink toy. With a flick of a switch, she activated it, and it began to vibrate enticingly. "There's nothing worse than these batteries dying in the middle," she groaned, testing a few more toys to ensure they were fully charged.

"Ah, this one," she said, her eyes landing on a sleek, purple toy that glimmered under the soft light. "You know, George? You're my favourite but I am naming you Kiaan for today. You're the one who always seems to understand my needs. Just like he gets me or at least listens to me." She spoke to the vibrating purple toy affectionately, a hint of humour lightening her mood.

Moments later, Mia found herself lost in sensations, her mind momentarily escaping the thoughts of Kiaan. She surrendered to the pleasure, feeling the frustration and confusion surrounding her feelings for him fade into the background, replaced by waves of bliss that washed over her.

"This is exactly what I needed," she sighed, letting out a soft moan as she let herself be carried away. With a satisfied smile lingering on her lips, Mia decided it was time to pamper herself further. She picked up her phone and dialled the spa. "Hello. This is Bathhouse Spa. How may I help you?" came the warm voice on the other end. "I was wondering if there's room for one person for a massage?" Mia asked, excitement bubbling within her. "Yes, which type?" the lady inquired.

"I'll take a full-body massage," Mia replied. "Ma'am, we have a cancellation for 11:30 am. Would you like to take this appointment?" the receptionist offered. "Perfect!" Mia said as she provided her details and hung up the phone. "It's like this man has a mansion in my mind," she muttered to herself, shaking off lingering thoughts of Kiaan as she slipped into a comfortable outfit and headed to the spa.

She entered and the soothing scent of lavender enveloped her, and she felt her tension begin to melt away. Mia settled into the waiting area, pulling out her phone to check for messages. She glanced at the screen for what felt like the hundredth time that morning. Still no message from Kiaan. Letting out a frustrated huff, she bit her lip.

"Why hasn't he texted me? What's taking him so long?" The thought of him being wrapped up in someone else's attention made her stomach churn.

"Players... all men are players," she muttered under her breath. "Glad there was no kiss," she recalled their last meeting—how he had looked at her with those deep, captivating eyes, attempting to kiss her lips. Lost in her thoughts, Mia closed her eyes and took a deep breath, trying to let go of her frustrations. Just then, a gentle voice broke through her reverie.

"Mia?" a woman called softly, her warm smile instantly putting Mia at ease. "I'm here to take you for your treatment." Mia nodded and followed the woman down the hall. The therapist led her into a beautifully decorated room, dimly lit by flickering candles.

The walls were adorned with soft, earthy tones, and the atmosphere was suffused with the sweet scent of red roses delicately arranged in a vase on the side table. A hot tub filled with steaming water bubbled invitingly in one corner, surrounded by more candles that cast a soft, romantic glow.

"Please, change into this," the woman said, gesturing towards a plush robe hanging on the door. "I'll step outside and send in our therapist." "Thank you," Mia replied, grateful for the privacy. Once alone, she quickly changed into the robe, feeling the soft fabric against her skin.

"Hello, Mia. I'm your massage therapist for today, and my name is Helen. How are you today?" The therapist entered, wearing blue scrubs, as Mia lay face down on the massage bed, her body sinking into the soft linens.

"I'm good, thank you," Mia replied, adjusting her position on the bed. "Okay, we are doing a 45-minute deep tissue massage. Please let me know if I'm too strong or too soft," the therapist said, her voice a soothing melody.

"Absolutely," Mia replied, closing her eyes and allowing herself to relax as Helen began the massage. The therapist's skilled hands worked magic over Mia's tense muscles. With each knead and stroke, she felt the weight of her worries dissipate, replaced by waves of tranquillity. "Just breathe and let go," Helen encouraged, her touch firm yet gentle. "You deserve this time for yourself." Mia nodded, a soft sigh escaping her lips.

"It feels amazing," she murmured, surrendering to the moment. After what felt like an eternity of bliss, the therapist finished the massage and gently tapped Mia's shoulder. "All done. How do you feel?" "Like I'm floating," Mia replied, a smile breaking through her earlier frustration.

"Thank you so much." "You're welcome! Now, if you'd like, you can relax in the hot tub," Helen suggested, gesturing towards the inviting tub. "I'll prepare some champagne for you," she added with a smile. "Champagne?" Mia's eyes lit up. "That sounds perfect." The therapist prepared the tub, and Mia slipped into the warm water, allowing the heat to envelop her.

The aroma of the candles wafted up, calming her already relaxed body. The therapist returned with a glass of champagne, the bubbles sparkling in the soft light. "Here you go," she said, handing the glass to Mia. "Enjoy." "Thank you," Mia said, lifting the glass to her lips.

She took a sip, the effervescence tickling her senses. "Mmm, this is wonderful." With a playful smile, she added, "You know, someone once said there's only one pain one should like, and that's champagne!" The therapist laughed, her eyes sparkling with amusement. "That's a great philosophy! Cheers to that!"

"Cheers!" Mia echoed, raising her glass before taking another sip, feeling the warmth of the champagne spread through her. "Okay, I will leave you and the champagne alone. Embrace yourself and have a great rest of your day," the therapist said, walking out the door and closing it gently behind her.

Mia remained in the hot tub, sipping on the champagne, but thoughts of Kiaan lingered in her mind. She couldn't shake the question: Should she text him or not? The uncertainty gnawed at her even as she tried to relax and enjoy the moment.

Message Sent!

A message from the heart!

Kiaan blinked against the harsh fluorescent lights of the hospital room, finally feeling more like himself after the ordeal. He sat up on the edge of the bed, hospital scrubs clinging to his frame. His chest hair peeked out, a reminder of his rugged charm, but today, he felt vulnerable.

"Nurse, can you please text for me? I have a fractured hand," he requested, his voice steady despite the discomfort. "Oh yes, for sure," the nurse replied, her tone professional yet warm. "Please just pull up the number for Mia, and I'll use a voice note. Thank you," Kiaan added, his heart racing at the thought of reaching out to her. The nurse nodded and quickly retrieved Mia's number from his records.

Kiaan took the phone, his fingers trembling slightly as he held down the record button. He took a deep breath, gathering his thoughts.

"Dear Mia," he began, his voice sincere, "I've only had three or four dates, and I don't even know if you're a doctor, an insurance agent, or a serial killer. But I want to say I love you. I'm in the hospital, and I'm getting discharged soon. If you have any feelings for me, please come visit me at my place. You know the address—where we played Minecraft. Yours, Kiaan." He hit send once the text was typed with the help of voice recognition, feeling a mix of relief and anxiety wash over him.

Just then, the door swung open and Kavya entered, her expression shifting from concern to surprise as she spotted the nurse. "Hey, is Kiaan okay?" Kavya asked, her voice laced with worry. The nurse smiled reassuringly. "He's awake and about to be discharged. Just wrapping up a few things."

"Great! I was so worried," Kavya said, her eyes darting to Kiaan, who was now sitting up straight, a hint of a smile playing on his lips. "Kiaan! You scared me," she said, moving closer. "How are you feeling?" "I'm good. Ready to get out of here," Kiaan replied, his gaze lingering on her as if trying to read her thoughts. Kavya glanced at the nurse, who was gathering Kiaan's belongings.

"Can I take him home?" she asked, her tone a mix of determination and concern. "Of course! Just sign these discharge papers, and you're all set," the nurse said, handing over a clipboard.

Kiaan signed; Kavya's heart raced. She felt a strange mix of emotions—relief, affection, and a flicker of something deeper. Once the paperwork was complete, Kiaan stood up carefully, testing his balance. Kavya offered him her arm for support. "Let's get you home," she said, her voice softening. They walked together out of the hospital, the cool air hitting them as they stepped outside. Kiaan spotted her car—an Uber waiting by the kerb. They got in, and Kavya turned to him, her expression serious.

"You really scared me, you know? I thought something terrible had happened." Kiaan chuckled lightly, trying to ease the tension, "I'm sorry. I guess I'm a bit of a magnet for trouble." Once they arrived at Kiaan's house, he felt a rush of nostalgia. The last time he had been here, everything felt different. The air was thick with unspoken words, but today, he was determined to change that. "Welcome back to your mansion," Kavya teased as they stepped inside, the living room still decorated from the New Year's party she had thrown for him.

"Welcome, Kiaan," his whole team screamed as they both entered.

"Kiaan!" John exclaimed, rushing forward and enveloping him in a tight hug. "We were so worried about you." Maria followed closely behind, her eyes glistening with tears. She stepped up to Kiaan and pressed a gentle kiss to his forehead. "You are like my son, Kiaan!" she cried, her voice thick with emotion. "It's okay, Maria. I'm fine," Kiaan reassured her, patting her back gently.

"Hey, everyone!" Kiaan called out, his voice steadying as he addressed the group. "Thank you all for being here. It means a lot to me." As the team settled back into a comfortable rhythm, they began to praise Kavya for taking care of Kiaan during his ordeal.

"You're a lifesaver, Kavya! We couldn't have asked for a better person to look after him," John said with a wide grin on his face. "Absolutely! You've done so much for him," Maria added, her voice warm and appreciative. Kavya felt a flush of warmth spread through her as they showered her with compliments. Kiaan, standing amidst his friends, turned to Kavya with genuine gratitude in his eyes. "Thank you, Kavya," he said, stepping closer to her.

Just then the doorbell rings. The music plays in the background and everyone looks at the door.

The End

John swung open the door, revealing Mia standing there, her expression a mix of determination and anxiety. She stepped inside, her eyes quickly scanned the room, landing on Kiaan, who was surrounded by his team. The atmosphere was charged with excitement and chatter, but Mia felt a different kind of tension in the air. "Mia? You?" Kavya said, taking a few steps forward, her surprise evident.

Kiaan's happy demeanour shifted slightly as he saw Kavya's expression. "You two know each other?" he asked, his brow furrowing in confusion. "She is my cousin," Mia replied, a hint of pride in her voice. "No, she's my kitchen helper," Kiaan countered, a mixture of bewilderment and amusement dancing in his eyes.

Mia rolled her eyes playfully. "She's my cousin and a celebrity with over a million followers. She could buy four more restaurants like yours in the city," she declared.

Kiaan turned to Kavya, his expression a cocktail of surprise and intrigue. "Is that true?" he asked, trying to process the information.

Kavya nodded, her cheeks flushing under the scrutiny. "She's right. I'm the one who left notes on your desk, and I sent you balloons because I love you," she confessed, her heart racing as she laid bare her feelings. Kiaan's eyes widened in shock.

"So, both of you knew what was going on the whole time, and I'm being played?" He sank onto the couch, running his hands through his hair in frustration.

"This is so confusing, man! Who loves whom here?" Jessi interjected, her voice cutting through the tension.

"I came here because Kiaan sent me this voicemail," Mia said, holding out her phone for Kavya to hear.

"The party is over. Everyone, please leave," Kiaan said, his voice taut with frustration. The team began to disperse. Kavya and Mia exchanged glances, silently agreeing to leave together.

They stepped outside into the crisp evening air and hailed a taxi. The silence between them was thick, filled with unspoken thoughts and emotions. "It isn't a game,

Mia. You should go tell him that you love him too," Kavya finally broke the silence, her voice soft but firm.

"What about you, Kav?" Mia questioned, concern etched on her face. Kavya chuckled lightly, "What about me? Am I the greatest actor in this drama? He could tell I wasn't just a dishwasher. Maybe I'll go back and make a movie out of this love story. It's a lot of drama no matter what!" She laughed, wrapping her arms around Mia in a tight hug.

"Driver, please make a U-turn and take us back!" Mia instructed the taxi driver, a newfound determination in her voice. The taxi turned back towards Kiaan's house. Kavya sat back, her heart pounding with anticipation and uncertainty.

Mia hopped out of the car as they arrived, her heart racing, and walked up to the door. She rang the doorbell, and Kiaan opened the door, surprise etched across his face. "Now what? Do you want to murder me? Who knows? You could be a serial killer too," he said, his tone laced with exasperation.

But Mia didn't hesitate. She dropped to her knees, looking up at him with earnest eyes.

"Kiaan, I want to adopt a girl and raise her with you." His expression shifted, curiosity piqued as he listened to her.

"I want to make love to you all night long with the windows open and the wind coming in from the sea," she continued, her voice steady and filled with emotion.

"I want to kiss on the beach under the bright light of the moon, falling on us. I want to walk with you in the cold rain and then jump in the hot tub and snuggle, with candles and a cognac drink." Kiaan's heart raced as he absorbed her words, feeling the weight of her affection.

"I want to sit by the bonfire with you and talk all night long with music playing in the background. I love you, Kiaan... love you to the moon and back... back and forth a million times."

Without thinking, Kiaan stepped forward, lifted Mia into his arms, and kissed her deeply on the lips. The world around them faded, leaving just the two of them in that moment of connection.

"Should I tell Kavya to leave? She's outside in a taxi," Mia asked, pulling back slightly, her cheeks flushed.

"Yes, and tell her she's fired," Kiaan replied, laughter breaking through his earlier frustration. They both chuckled, the tension dissipating as they embraced the warmth of their mutual feelings, ready to face whatever came next together.

"Thank you Jay and Panda for always being there."

www.ingramcontent.com/pod-product-compliance
Lightning Source LLC
LaVergne TN
LVHW041202150826
845673LV00001B/257

* 9 7 9 8 8 9 6 9 9 2 8 3 7 *